I0689503
2
NOVELLAS

Advance Praise for

WOMEN BORN WITH FUR

"A memorable and singular debut."
—**Peter Markus,** author of *The Fish and the Not Fish*

An intoxicating book and brew."
—**Frederick Barthelme,** author of *Waveland* and *There Must Be Some Mistake*

"Sly and brilliant."
—**Lidia Yuknavitch,** author of *The Chronology of Water* and *Dora: A Headcase*

"Utterly heartbreaking."
—**Courtney Eldridge,** author of *Unkempt* and *The Generosity of Women*

+

Advance Praise for

OUT FROM THE PLEIADES

"A rollicking, raucous, new myth. A classic."
—**Susanne Antonetta,** author, *Make Me a Mother: a memoir*, and *Body Toxic: An Environmental Memoir*

"Marked by McGrath's signature wit, compassion and insight."
—**Bruce Snider,** poet, *Paradise, Indiana*, Lena-Miles Wever Todd Poetry Prize; and *The Year We Studied Women*, Felix Pollak Prize in Poetry

"A rich romp, chockfull of feel-good details."
—**Amy King,** poet, *I Want to Make You Safe* and *I'm the Man Who Loves You*

Our Blue Bustard series presents two novellas, each by a different author, in one beautifully illustrated book and ebook, published by Jaded Ibis Press.
Black-and-white editions are published individually.

In this edition:

Women Born with Fur
a biographical novella by
Beth Couture
Begins on Page 5

+

Out from the Pleiades
a picaresque novella in verse by
Leslie McGrath
Begins on Page 95

2 NOVELLAS

WOMEN BORN WITH FUR

A BIOGRAPHY

BETH COUTURE

Jaded Ibis Press
sustainable literature by digital means™
an imprint of Jaded Ibis Productions
Seattle • Hong Kong • Boston

hypertrichosis:
growth of hair in excess
of the normal.

1: CHILDHOOD

Nualli

A woman gives birth to a baby girl covered in fur—her arms and legs and face, her entire body. It is like hair, only thicker, coarser, with an under layer like what animals have to keep themselves warm in the winter. The only parts of the baby's body that aren't covered are her palms and the soles of her feet. The woman looks at the baby for a long time, holds it carefully in her arms until the moon is high, and then she places her on the ground under a tree. It is cold, and even though the child is wrapped in a wool blanket, the woman can see her shiver. But she doesn't cry. The woman is amazed and frightened by the child, because she has not cried at all. The woman thinks of the birth—squatting down, holding her hands underneath her to catch the baby, grunting, the smell of blood and placenta, body smells she had never known before. She screamed with pain, but the baby didn't make a sound, not even after she cleaned its nose and mouth, after she held it upside down and slapped its back. Part of her wished it would be dead when she saw it, but the baby breathed. Her little girl. A curse. She can't go back to her home now, not with this child wrapped in blankets, her tiny furry hands clenched in fists, her dark eyes staring at her mother, at everything around her. The woman knows what they will say, and so she must leave the child here in the cold and hope that her death comes as easily as her birth. She tucks the blanket around the baby's face, under her chin

and over her ears. She places a tiny piece of milk candy in the child's mouth so that she will have some sweetness before she dies. The baby watches her as she walks back toward home.

Birth

Mary's older sisters threaten to take vials of her blood and mail them to zoologists to have them tested. There is something really wrong, and once their parents find out the truth, they say, they'll send her back and get the daughter they should have gotten in the first place. One with curly red hair and freckles, and maybe a dimple in her right cheek. They show Mary photographs of herself as a baby, face and body covered in thick dark fur. Like hair, only not. It's fur. The distinction is obvious even in the photographs. Mary can't believe she was ever so small. She runs her fingers over the fur on her arms, rubs it against her face. In the photographs, her mother holds Mary up to the camera, feeds her, watches as Mary's father tickles the baby's feet. In at least one of them her mother is smiling.

Infancy

(Mary's sisters hold her down and prick her with needles. They squeeze her skin until the blood drips into a small plastic cup with a pink dinosaur on it—Mary's drinking cup—and then they put a piece of masking tape with the words "Mary's blood" on it around the lip of the cup. Mary screams and struggles, and though she is a baby, she is nearly as strong as Lula and Mel, and when her baby fists make contact with their arms and faces, they hurt.

"What are you doing to the baby?" Mary's mother asks as

she walks quickly into the room, her face angry and concerned. "What are you doing to her?" She picks Mary up and shushes her, bounces her on her hip.

"We were just playing," Lula says, and elbows Mel in the ribs, gives her a look. "She just started screaming for no reason." Mel nods.

"You can't be so rough with her," Mary's mother says, and pats Mary's rear end through her diaper. Mary gets quiet, but looks wary. "You have to be gentle."

"Sorry, Mom," Lula says, and if her mother were looking she would be able to tell that Lula isn't sorry at all, but she's not looking. She's watching Mary as Mary watches her, her dark eyes wide and full of tears. She brushes her lips against the fur on Mary's forehead and looks at her other daughters, at their perfect pale skin, their perfect cruel hands.)

Toys

Mary's sisters hate her, but while she is very little, they play with her all the time. They dress her up in too-small doll clothes and drag her through the yard, put her in the tallest trees they can climb and refuse to take her down until she starts screaming and they are afraid someone will hear her. Mel always flinches first, and pulls her down, then pats her back and strokes her arms until she stops crying. They call her their toy, their stuffed animal, and even make a leash for her out of braided yarn. Mel is sometimes nice to her and feeds her bits of cookie or candy, things their parents don't want her to have, but Mary is terrified of her sisters even when they are kind. The smell of strawberry bubblegum on their mouths makes her feel sick, and she hates their sticky hands on her fur. Whenever they come near her, she cries. But when she gets too heavy for them to carry around, they ignore her, and this is worse. She learns how to walk and follows them from room to room, leaves her toys in their beds, tries to give them her food. Sometimes she crawls on hands and knees over to them and barks, or rubs against their legs. Her father plays along and scratches her head, behind her ears, and calls her a good girl, but her sisters just look at her. Lula rolls her eyes. "Cut it out," she says, "you're too ugly to be a dog." Mary's mother swats Lula when she says this, tells her to apologize to Mary, and Lula always does.

Holidays

It is Christmas, and Mary's father is decorating the tree with garland and tinsel and small wooden ornaments shaped like stars and boats and houses. Her mother is sitting on the couch directing him, telling him to move this strand of garland that way and that ornament from this branch to another. Her father does what he is told, and pretty soon all of the ornaments are on the tree. Her mother and father sit down next to each other, and Mary clambers up onto the couch to sit in between them. Lula and Mel are fighting over who gets to put the angel on top, and so far Lula is winning. Her father plays with both Mary's and her mother's ponytails, tapping first one, then the other, and saying "ding-dong, ding-dong" in a deep silly voice. Her mother leaves the next year, taking the box of wooden ornaments and the angel with her.

Mary's Mother

After she leaves, people will say it was because of Mary, that she couldn't stand having such a daughter, a freak, a little girl who looked like a monkey. Not when she was so beautiful, so dark and slender and dignified, when she could walk into a room and you stopped what you were doing and looked, because you felt she deserved it. "Like a monkey," they will say, and shake their heads. They will say this, will say "it's no wonder" when they see Mary and her father and sisters in the grocery store or the K-Mart, "who can blame her with a daughter like that?" but this is not why she leaves. As she packs her things and gets into the car, she will think about taking Mary with her—not the others, just Mary—but then, she doesn't even know where she's going and so it wouldn't be fair. She has some money, but it will run out. She could work as a secretary, but she has no other skills. Things will be tough for a while. Her husband isn't much, but he will at least take care of Mary, and he will always be there. She knows she can depend on him. So she goes, thinks maybe one day she will come back for her daughter. She doesn't know where she's going, but she knows it must be far away, and she knows her husband won't come looking for her. They understand each other, she thinks. But the night before she goes, she stands in Mary's room watching her daughter sleep. She wants to remember her face.

Mary's Mother

(She didn't leave because of Mary. This is what everyone says, but they're full of shit. Mary's mother left because she was bored. She left because of the other two, the older, crueler daughters. She left because she didn't know what else to do. But Mary will always wonder if her mother left because of her, and she will always wonder what things would have been like if her mother had stayed. She will want to look for her mother, but she won't know where to start.)

Learning

The boys at school won't leave her alone, and to keep them from bothering her, Mary hits and bites at them every time they come near her. One day Richie Freeman gets too close and ends up with a broken nose and bites on his arm, and Mary is sent to the principal's office. Mary looks out the window while the principal talks to her. He tells her he will be calling her father to come get her and take her home for three days' suspension. She watches snow falling on the kids outside playing, their mouths open as they shout, showing red gums and sharp white teeth.

Richie will have to get a tetanus shot, and he will never look at Mary again. When she passes him in the hallway, or even when someone mentions her, Richie will stare at the scars on his arm, will run his fingers over the bump on the bridge of his nose and won't say a word. Though he will never tell anyone, when he is grown up Richie will sometimes touch his scars with his tongue, will try to remember the feel of Mary's fingernails on his skin. When someone asks him how he broke his nose he will tell them he did it playing football, and they will know he is lying but won't bother to ask him the truth.

the giant is in love
with Mary but he likes
to watch the girl in the Stetson
and imagines fucking her

Parents

When Mary's mother left, she didn't tell any of them where she was going. She packed up her small car with as much as it could hold, told Mary and her sisters to be good, and drove away. Mary's father gets checks from her once in a while, but never anything else. Sometimes Lula and Mel get birthday cards with glitter inside, pop-up cards with zoo animals and clowns. Mary gets cards too, but they have delicate flowers on them, constellations, strange beautiful people with the bodies of animals. In Lula's and Mel's, Mary's mother always writes "Love, Mom." Nothing else. In Mary's, she draws pictures, tapes feathers and small flat stones. The postmarks on the envelopes are never from the same place. Mary doesn't remember much about her mother, and so she looks at photographs to remind her. There is a garbage bag full of them in the garage, and she sits on the cold concrete floor digging through them, running her fingers over the faces—her own, her sisters', her mother's.

There is one photograph that Mary can't stand—it is one of her mother alone, standing in the driveway next to a wide blue car. She is laughing, head thrown back and eyes closed, and her hand rests on the roof of the car as if to support her. Her dark hair is under a blue scarf, but strands of it have escaped and brush against her face. It is winter—the sky is white behind her and all the trees are bare, and Mary's mother wears a cream-colored sweater and a heavy wool coat. Her pregnant belly strains against her clothes. If it weren't for this, she could be a model in a catalogue. Mary thinks her mother is the loveliest thing she's ever seen. She has to hold herself back from scratching holes in the photograph, from tearing it apart completely.

Pets

1.

When Mary is eight years old, her father brings home an orange and white kitten from the animal shelter for her and her sisters. Lula and Mel wanted a dog, but Dad says cats are cleaner and don't need as much attention. Because Lula is the oldest, she gets to name the kitten. She deliberates for days, and finally decides to call him Ben. Ben likes Mary because she leaves him alone. She never grabs and squeezes him like her sisters do. The kitten sleeps in Mary's bed every night, and sometimes she wakes up to Lula or Mel feeling around in the dark for him so they can take him back to their room. The kitten hisses when they touch him, and hides under the bed until they leave. After a while, Mel and Lula forget about him, and he is Mary's cat. He leaves pale fur on her clothes and her bed, and she often wakes up to him curled on her pillow, his paws in her face. He purrs whenever she touches him. Sometimes he sits up all night watching her from the top of her bookshelf. Mary imagines he's trying to protect her.

2.

Pretty soon, Mary's sisters get the puppy they've wanted. They whine and cry and beg until their father gives in, and one night after dinner they all have to go together to the pet store. Lula refuses to get a shelter dog. She says they have too many diseases, and she saw a show on TV when she was spending the night at Molly Kelly's house about shelter dogs being twenty five percent more likely to attack their owners than dogs you buy at a pet store. "And that animal shelter is gross," she says. "Molly's parents brought their dog there after it bit Molly's brother, and they told her the smell was so bad they'd never go there again." Mary can tell her father isn't listening to Lula anymore, but he says "okay, sweetie" every time she pauses. He looks out the window at other cars as he drives and taps his fingers on the wheel in time to the sound of the windshield wipers.

At the pet store, Lula and Mel stick their fingers through the holes in the puppy cages and giggle when the puppies bite at them. Mel likes a cocker spaniel that whines and yips whenever anyone gets near it, but Lula tells her that cocker spaniels grow up to be fat and lazy and they should get a schnauzer. Mary watches them until she gets bored, and then she goes over to the reptile tanks. The snakes have just been fed, and a small pink corn snake struggles to swallow a baby mouse whole. Mary watches the small dark form move down the snake's body. She imagines she can hear it squeak from inside the snake's stomach.

Lula and Mel decide on their puppy, and Lula carries it around in her arms while they pick out a sparkly pink collar, a pink and purple striped dog bed with "Princess" stamped in rhinestones on its front, and a collection of stuffed toys. The puppy tries to wriggle out of Lula's grasp, but she holds it tight against her chest and then it just whines. When they finally leave the store, it has stopped raining. Lula attaches the puppy's new leash to her collar and lets the puppy walk through the parking lot. It drinks from a puddle, then squats to pee next to their car.

3.

Ben is hit by a car eight months later, and Mary helps her father bury him in the backyard. Her father digs the hole, but it is Mary's job to collect the rocks and pieces of root out of it and throw them away. Her sisters watch from the living room window. When her father goes back inside, Mary sits with her hands in the dirt until it is dark, and then she can't see where she ends and the ground begins.

Pet

The men find the baby under a tree, wrapped in a rough wool blanket and nearly frozen. It is not dead, and they are surprised that its heart still beats, surprised when weak puffs of air can still be seen coming from its lips. At first they think it is an animal, a monkey or a gorilla, but they examine it, and it is a little girl. They wonder what they should do with it, and though they want to leave it where it is, they know their wives would kill them. A baby is a baby, after all, even if it looks like it belongs in the trees. One of them wraps the creature in his coat, and they carry it to the hospital. "It isn't ours," they say, "one of the Indians must have left it there to die." They talk about savages. The nurses understand. The one who carried the child in his arms wants to wait to learn if she will live, but the others refuse. "We did everything we could," they say. "We've wasted our day already." They are meant to be surveying the land, determining if it will be good ground for planting. It isn't. They will tell the Queen this. Still, the one who carried her insists, says he will catch up with the others. When the doctor finds him, tells him the baby will survive ("though to lead what kind of life, I can't be sure"), the man prepares to go. He should find his colleagues, must have some dinner and perhaps a brandy. He hesitates.

"But what will you do with her?" he asks the doctor.

"There are plenty of orphanages," the doctor says. The man nods.

"But if someone wished to adopt her now? After she recovers, I mean?"

"The chances of someone wanting to adopt this particular baby are quite slim, I'm afraid." The doctor turns to go, then turns around again. "Then again, the fur might all fall out on its own. I have heard of such

things happening. She's an Indian, so it's hard to tell what might happen, but it is possible. And she is healthy, surprisingly robust for such a young child. She can be barely a day old, and for her to have survived all night in the cold, with no food, well, it's quite shocking."

The man doesn't know what he's saying anymore. He is tired, hungry, exhausted from the day. He carried her to the hospital. He heard her breathe easier as she settled into his coat, soothed by the warmth from his body. This child has claimed him.

He clears his throat. "May I come to see her? Is it allowed?"

The doctor looks at him strangely, as if trying to make sense of him, and then shrugs. "If you wish. Give her a day or two so she is completely out of danger before you come."

"Of course."

When he goes home, he tells his wife about the child. They have not had children of their own, something they never expected to regret, but do, despite never speaking of it. He tells her it would be easy to adopt her, so much easier than if she were a normal child. "No one else will take her," he says, "but she deserves a home like anyone else, doesn't she? The doctor says the hair—the fur—might just fall out on its own anyway. She's healthy, and normal otherwise." She is hesitant at first (he has been honest about the baby's appearance; how could he not be?), but he can tell she is warming to the idea. She says as soon as they are able to, she will go with him to see the child.

Ghosts

Mary can no longer see Ben, but she knows he has come back. She knows he is near her. She can feel his weight, and the bed is warm in the spot where he used to sleep. Sometimes she smells him—his fur, the fishy tang of his breath. If she listens closely enough, she

there are feathers
and rhinestones
in the woman's hair

can hear him purring. Sometimes at night, she wakes up with the feeling of a cat on her chest, and when she strokes the air with her hand something changes in it. It feels warmer, more alive. She gets used to this, and she no longer misses him so much. She still talks to him when she feels like it, only now she's careful that no one hears her. She tries to leave food out for him, but her father catches her and tells her not to be wasteful. Her sisters cry over Ben—Lula sobs and says it was all her fault; she should have been more responsible and should never have let him go outside, and Mel goes out to the grave in the backyard almost every day. They ignore the puppy, because it makes them feel guilty. "Poor Ben," they say, sighing heavily. "Poor, poor little cat." Mary wants to hit them when they say this, but she wonders if maybe they really are sad, if maybe they feel regret. She knows they must feel something, because otherwise they wouldn't cry so much. She wonders if she should tell them what she knows, that Ben isn't really gone and they could feel him like she can if they tried. In the end she decides against it.

Puberty

When Mary turns thirteen, her sisters decide to shave her. She tries to fight them, but they are bigger than her, and they force her to take off her clothes and get into the shower while they look for their father's Bic razor and shaving cream. Mel smears her with shaving cream while Lula wets the razor and begins to shave Mary, starting with her chest. Mary tries to cover her small breasts with her hands, but Lula bats them away. "I'm not going to cut off your little titties," she says. She has to go over some sections of fur two or three times before she gets it all, and the razor leaves little red bumps all over Mary's skin. Matted clumps of fur gather at her feet. It takes her sisters over an hour, and when they are done, the only hair left on Mary's body is on her head. The rest of her body is marble pale and shivering. When her sisters leave the bathroom, Mary stands in front of the mirror trying to figure out her skin.

A Miracle

The next morning, the fur has returned, and it is healthier and more plentiful than ever before. Mary lies in bed and rolls from side to side, pleased with the way her body feels against the flannel sheets. She can hardly believe she was even shaved in the first place. There is no sign that she was ever hairless, that her sisters even touched her. She thinks she must have dreamed it, but she can smell Barbasol when she lifts her arms to stretch, and when she sniffs herself, it is stronger. When she showers, the smell of the shaving cream is washed away, and all that is left is her own warm, sweet smell. She stays in the shower until Mel bangs on the door and tells her to hurry up, then she dries off and puts on her favorite t-shirt and jeans, victorious.

Unbelievers

When Mary comes down to the table, her sisters and father are already sitting there. Mel and Lula eat cereal that dyes the milk in their bowls purple, and their father drinks coffee from a large mug with a tooth on it that he got from the dentist's office. When Lula and Mel see Mary, they stop eating and stare at her, then they look at each other. Mary smiles at them and sits down, pours milk and cereal into her favorite bowl.

"Aren't you girls going to be late?" their father asks them a few minutes later, looking at his watch, but Lula and Mel don't answer. They are watching Mary eat, looking back and forth between her and each other. He sighs and pours the rest of his coffee down the sink. "You're going to be late," he says, and Lula and Mel finally look at him and get up from the table. On the way to school, they won't talk to Mary. They walk together in front of her, leaving her behind, and she hears them talking about her. "It's embarrassing," Lula says, and Mel nods, her ponytail bobbing up and down. Mary walks behind them listening and doesn't try to catch up.

A Miracle

(The next morning, Mary is covered in short, stubbly fur. Her body itches. When she looks in the mirror, her skin is gray, like her father's when he hasn't shaved in a while. *Five o'clock shadow*, she thinks. The tiny thin needles of fur prick her fingers when she touches her arms and stomach, her chest. She can't go to school looking like this, and so she asks Mel to tell their father she is sick. He comes upstairs to check on her, but she says he can't come in. "I have cramps," she says when he knocks on the door, "Go away. I have my period." He doesn't say anything, and she hears him walk away. After two more days, her fur has grown out enough so that it looks normal again, and Mary goes to school. Her sisters don't say anything about what happened, and neither does she.)

The Real Miracle that isn't a Miracle at all

(Mary wakes up the morning after her sisters shave her and there is blood on her sheets. Her body itches and is covered in stubble, like when her father hasn't shaved in a few days. She can't go anywhere looking like this, and besides, she feels horrible. Her stomach and back hurt, and she thinks she might throw up. Mel comes in to wake her, and sees the sheets, the blood on Mary's nightgown. She calls for Lula, and the two of them bring Mary into the bathroom, try to clean her up.

"It's just your period," Lula says, giving Mary a large Always pad in a green wrapper. "Put this in your underwear. You'll be fine." Mary does as she's told, and Lula goes downstairs to tell their father that Mary's sick.

"Don't tell him the truth," Mary says, and Lula rolls her eyes.

"Of course not," she says.

Mary's father comes upstairs to check on her, and when he comes into the room, she is lying in bed reading a magazine. Mel has changed the sheets, and Mary is clean and comfortable, if a bit crampy.

"Will you be okay alone today?" her father asks, and Mary nods. "I can stay home if you need me to," he says.

"I'll be fine," she says, and he smiles at her.

When Lula and Mel get home from school, they come up to Mary's room. She is asleep, and they tap her on the shoulder until she wakes up.

"We brought you something," Lula says, and Mel holds out a candy bar. "Girls on their periods always like chocolate," Mel says.

Birthday

In another photograph, Mary's mother is wearing a flowered summer dress and is standing at the kitchen counter frosting a cake. Mary is sitting in a yellow high chair holding a spoon. She watches her mother. Mary doesn't remember that day, but she knows it was her second birthday. There are snapshots of the birthday party, too—they show Mary wearing a pink hat and batting at a large balloon, her sisters watching her with bored expressions, and Mary digging at a piece of cake with her fingers while her mother tries to clean her face with her bib. In the last photo, Mary is screaming, beating the table with angry fists. Her face, shirt, and fur are smeared with pink frosting and chocolate cake, and Lula is laughing in the background. Mel looks like she is going to cry. Both sisters have cake and frosting in their hands. In front of Mary, her mother looks directly at the camera, her face tired. Mary wonders how far away she was even then.

The Doctor

Her sisters won't stop nagging her father to take Mary to a doctor. They say there must be some sort of hormonal imbalance, perhaps it's hereditary, and they have a right to know if there's something really wrong with her. They say their own children, if they ever have them, might be at risk. When this doesn't work, Lula tries a different tactic and says that Mary will be happier without all that fur covering her, that a young girl needs to feel attractive and desirable in order to succeed. She tells their father that he is doing Mary a disservice by not trying to get her help. Mary overhears them talking, and she tries to tell her father that everything is fine, she doesn't need a doctor, but her sisters tell her not to be so stupid. Mary bares her teeth at them, holds back a growl.

At the doctor's office, Mary is given blood tests, urine tests, skin swabs, and laser treatments. The office is clean and white and quiet, and Mary likes sitting on the examination table so much that when it is time to leave, her father has to take her by the arm to get her to climb down. She kicks her feet against the table and tells him she wants to stay. She asks the doctor to give her more tests, to examine strands of her fur under the microscope, but he smiles and shakes his head. They find nothing wrong with her—in fact, she is healthier than anyone else in her family. The doctor says that the fur will likely fall out as she gets older, that he firmly believes that Mary will live a perfectly normal life. Later, in bed, Mary can't sleep without the light on. She keeps one hand on the lamp all night.

Definitions

Hypertrichosis: An excessive growth of hair on the body, possibly as a result of endocrine dysfunction, as in the hirsutism accompanying excessive adrenocortical function.

Hypertrichosis: Specifically refers to hair density or length beyond the accepted limits of normal for a particular age, race, or sex, and may be generalized or localized, and may be lanugo, vellus, or terminal hair.

Hypertrichosis: "Excessive hair growth at inappropriate locations, such as on the extremities, the head, and the back." It is caused by genetic or acquired factors, and is an androgen-independent process. This concept does not include hirsutism which is an

she loves the way
her fur feels
against his skin

androgen-dependent excess hair growth in women and children.

Hypertrichosis: Growth of hair in excess of the normal.

Hypertrichosis: A girl is born with hair, no, fur covering her entire body, everywhere but her palms and the bottoms of her feet. Everyone calls it hair, but she knows it is fur. The doctor calls it hair and says it will fall out when she is older, but she refuses to believe him. Fur and hair are not the same things. She is only a child, but even she knows this.

Fur: 1. The thick coat of soft hair covering the skin of a mammal, such as a fox or beaver.
2. The hair-covered, dressed pelt of such a mammal, used in the making of garments and as trimming or decoration.
3. A garment made of or lined with the dressed pelt of a mammal.
4. A coating similar to the pelt of a mammal.

Fur: 1. A piece of the dressed pelt of an animal used to make, trim, or line wearing apparel.
2.   An article of clothing made of or with fur.
3.   The hairy coat of a mammal especially when fine, soft, and thick; also: such a coat with the skin.
4.   A coating resembling fur: as **a:** a coat of ephithelial debris on the tongue. **b:** the thick pile of a fabric (as chenille).

Fur: 1. The soft, thick hair covering the body of many mammals.
2.   The skin bearing such hair, when stripped and processed for making, lining, or trimming garments; dressed pelt.
3.   Any garment, neckpiece, trimming, etc. made of such skins.

4. Any furlike or fuzzy coating, as diseased matter on the tongue in illness.

Fur: 1. The short, fine, soft hair of certain animals, growing thick on the skin, and distinguished from the hair, which is longer and coarser.
2. The skins of certain wild animals with the fur; peltry; as, a cargo of furs.
3. Strips of dressed skins with fur, used on garments for warmth or for ornament.
4. Articles of clothing made of fur; as, a set of furs for a lady (a collar, tippet, or cape, muff, etc.).
5. Any coating considered as resembling fur; as: a coat of morbid matter collected on the tongue in persons affected with fever.

Fur: There have been many women born with fur.

Obedience

Julia is nearly sixteen now, and her adoptive father has decided he needs money. His wife has been dead for eight years, and while Julia tries to take care of the household, she does not do a good job. She is too scattered, he tells her, too academic. She sits on the sofa and reads when she should be dusting the furniture. She practices her singing when she should be writing down instructions for dinner. He is grateful to her—she is a comfort to him—but there are days when he wonders how he could have been so impractical as to take in a foundling like her. His wife had loved her. She doted on the girl, gave her beautiful dresses and jewelry, treated her like their very own daughter. And Julia had loved her in return. But she is gone now, and the finances are poor. There are servants to pay, parties to throw. He is a man with social connections. This means there must be money. Julia's father would never make his adopted daughter work for a living. She would never do as a shop girl or a governess. She tutored a prominent family's children in Latin and French for a time, but the children could never fully move past her appearance. Their parents finally regretted it, they said, but they needed someone who would offer fewer distractions. And so Julia has remained at home ever since. But her father's inheritance has dwindled.

There is someone who has offered to take care of Julia, to give her anything she wants in exchange for the privilege of showing her to the public. She is an entertainer by nature, this man said after hearing her sing, and the world deserves to experience her talents. Julia and her father have discussed it. He can tell she doesn't wish to go with this man Lent, but he also knows she will if he asks her to. She has always been obedient, and he is grateful to her for this.

Loyalty

Mary's oldest sister has a boyfriend, a tall blonde skater punk named Kyle. He isn't supposed to be in the house, but he comes home with Lula every day after school and leaves before Mary's father gets home from work. They usually stay in Lula's bedroom until it is time for Kyle to leave, and Mary does her homework in the living room with the television on so she can't hear them. One afternoon he leaves early, and when he slams the front door behind him, Mary knows he isn't coming back. When Mary walks down the hall to the bathroom, she hears Lula crying in her room. She sounds like she'll never stop. That night she doesn't come out of her room, not for dinner, or even when Mary's father says he'll take her to the mall. Mary goes outside and collects broken bottles, sticks, a dead blue jay and a pile of its feathers, and brings them to Kyle's house. She leaves them on his porch. When she walks by the next morning, everything she left is gone—there's not even a trace. She passes the house, and is almost to the end of the street when she hears someone calling her name. It's Kyle.

"Hey," he says, jogging up to her.

"Hey," Mary says back, but she doesn't look at him.

"You're the one who left all that stuff on my porch," he says, and Mary knows he's telling her, not asking.

"You dumped my sister," she says.

"Why do you care anyway?" he asks.

"She's been crying all night, and she won't come out of her room."

"She cries all the time anyway," he says, "about everything."

"You're right," Mary says. "But she's really upset."

"Listen, my dad found what you left. He asked if it was some sort of cult stuff, Satanic or something." Kyle laughs a little when he says this. "I told him it was just a joke." He looks at Mary for a few seconds, then puts his hand on her arm. "I've always wondered what it feels like," he says, lightly stroking her fur. "It's not like regular hair at all." He pets her like he's petting a dog, gently and affectionately, until Mary pulls her arm away.

"I'm sorry about leaving that stuff," she says.

"It's cool," Kyle says. He looks at her arms until she pulls the sleeves of her jacket down to hide them.

"Are you going to call Lula?" Mary asks him. "You should."

"Yeah, I might call her," Kyle says, "if you think she'll answer the phone."

"Probably," Mary says.

"Do you want to hang out sometime?" Kyle asks her as she turns to walk away.

"Not really," Mary says.

That night, Kyle calls Lula and apologizes. Mary can hear Lula yelling at him over the phone, then speaking softly, giggling. The next day he comes over, and the day after that. He pretends not to see Mary, and she does the same for him.

Richie

He isn't in love with her. How could he be in love with a girl like that? Richie is attractive, a tall, wiry boy with strong arms and legs, blue eyes all the girls call "piercing." He is smart, but he doesn't like to show it, and when he sits in class with his arms folded, baseball cap pulled down over his eyes, he wonders what his life would be like if he decided to try, if he raised his hand or bothered to do his homework. He'll never do it, but sometimes he wants to. Sometimes he thinks he'll get out of this town, but fifteen years will go by, twenty, then thirty, and he'll still be here.

He isn't in love with Mary, he couldn't be, but he dreams about her. He imagines them standing side by side, her small hand in his large one. He'll imagine what she looks like under the fur, like it is a sweater she can take off, and he imagines touching her on her shoulder, her side, the small of her back. When he is fifteen and loses his virginity to the school's head cheerleader, he imagines he is on top of Mary instead, and this frightens him. He can't stop thinking about it, not even after he has slept with ten of the cheerleaders (the pretty ones), the girls' gymnastics team, and his 11th grade English teacher. Ms. Fuller is tall and red haired, and Richie's friends all fantasize about her. They look down her shirt when she leans over them to explain passages in *Macbeth* and watch her ass move from side to side as she erases the board. After she has sex with Richie in the backseat of her car, she resigns from her job and moves away.

Richie doesn't tell anyone what happened between them, doesn't tell anyone that he ran his hands through her long red hair and imagined it was fur, that he bit her lips and begged her to bite him back, to make his mouth bleed.

Kiss

Mary watches her sisters dance with their friends at her sixteenth birthday party and eats a piece of chocolate cake with her fingers. She sits on the stairs where no one can see her, but no one even looks for her. Lula and Mel seem to be having a good time, and Mary is glad. Their father has never allowed them to have a party before. He comes into the living room every few minutes with sodas or potato chips, but he doesn't say anything to anyone. When it is time to open gifts, Mary has to come downstairs. She opens box after box and says "thank you" without looking closely at their contents. The kids don't pay much attention to her, because Lula talks so much. She laughs and crunches chips, talks with her mouth full. When Mary finishes with the last box, she hears a boy's voice telling her to look up. She does, and is blinded by the flash of a camera. When she can see again, the boy is walking toward her, and he hands her a developing Polaroid photograph. She watches as her face appears, first yellow and fuzzy, then darker and more defined. Her mouth is open slightly and her lips are pursed like she is getting ready to blow a kiss to the boy taking the picture. She looks surprised, but almost happy. After everyone goes home, Mary leaves her presents downstairs for her sisters to go through and takes the photograph with her to her bedroom. She scratches the words *First Kiss* on the back of it with a ballpoint pen.

The Show

Julia and Lent are happy. He buys her all the dresses she could ever want and pays for singing lessons from some of the top teachers in England. He compliments her, tells her she had better be careful, because soon he's going to elope with her, sling her over his shoulder and carry him away to be his wife. Julia writes to her father, invites him to her performances. He has not come, and she rarely gets a reply to her letters. When she does, she can tell he has been drinking. She sends him money—a few pounds here, a few there, but he keeps asking for more until she is sending it to him every week. Lent tells her she cannot afford to support her father in the manner she does, but he doesn't forbid it.

Each night, Julia performs. She puts on one of her dresses—usually a bright yellow or pink one, something to show off her figure—and sings and dances, sometimes performs skits, adaptations of Shakespeare, for her adoring audience. They cheer for her, throw flowers onto the stage, are amazed by her talent. She has even had men propose to her, tell her they think her fur is attractive, handsome even. They say it makes her seem more womanly, softer, and somehow more innocent. Some say they will never look at a furless woman again. The men often want to touch her, to stroke her arms, her face; some even dare to ask to put their hand on her knee. Lent allows them only so much, and he makes them pay dearly for it. He gets jealous when a man pays too much attention to her, and Julia finds it charming. She wants to tell him he has nothing to worry about, that he is the only man she thinks of, but she feels sure he knows.

I love my fur...

2: TRAVELING

Leaving Home

Mary leaves home for the first time at nineteen, because she is sick of her father's house, sick of watching television every night and listening to her sisters argue on the phone with their boyfriends. She has no other reasons for going, no plans. She decides to hitch hike across the Midwest to California, or at least Colorado. As she packs her duffel bag, she imagines meeting a man to travel with, one who tells her stories about the people he knows, ones she reminds him of, a man who will stroke her face and head to help her fall asleep and will buy her French vanilla coffees and candy bars from gas stations while she waits in the car. She thinks about making it to a small town near the coast and working in an ice cream shop, of buying a tiny house that smells like old books and salt. Mary's first night on the road no one stops for her, so she walks until she can't anymore and then she sleeps in someone's yard. A dog wakes her up the next day by licking her hand, and it lets her pet it until its owners call it inside.

Leaving Home

(Mary leaves home for the first time at nineteen, because of the book. It's a small book, thin, almost like a pamphlet. She finds it in the mailbox wrapped in brown paper with no return address, but it smells like her mother's perfume, like what Mary imagines her mother's bedroom smells like. *Julia Pastrana*, the cover says, and Mary doesn't know if this is the author's name or the title of the book. She learns that it's the title, and that the book is about a woman named Julia who was also covered in fur. The author calls it "hair," not fur, but Mary can tell from the pictures that she and Julia are alike, and so Julia has fur. It makes a difference to her. She reads the book in an hour, sitting at the kitchen table with a cup of tea that gets cold, listening to rain on the roof. Julia lived in England in the 1800s, was a circus performer. Her manager married her, and when she died, he had her and her dead baby (also furry) stuffed and carried them on display all around the world. Now she's in a museum somewhere, or a hospital, somewhere in Europe. The author didn't know where, but speculated Oslo.

Mary thinks about the stuffed animals her father used to bring down in garbage bags from the attic—some were missing eyes or limbs, with saw dust and cotton stuffing falling out of the holes that mice had chewed in them. He would put them on the floor in the living room and tell Mary and her sisters to look through them and make sure they didn't want to keep any of them before he brought them to Goodwill or threw them out. "We need to start getting rid of some of this stuff," he'd say. Lula made Mel dig in the bags for her. She said the toys were filthy and she hated the way they felt on her hands. She made Mel pick out stuffed animals one by one, to hold them up and show them to her like she was trying to sell them, and never decided to keep anything. Their father would take the garbage bags into the garage, and they would sit there until he brought them back up into the attic. A few months later, he would bring down the same bags and tell the girls again to look through them in case there was anything they wanted. Mary never took things from the bags while her sisters were watching, but sometimes she would go into the garage and look through them herself, holding stuffed rabbits and horses and frogs in her lap, bringing them up to her nose and breathing in the smell of mildew and sawdust, and then returning them to the bags. She buried a stuffed sheep once, because she couldn't stand the idea of putting it back in plastic.)

First Love

Mary's second night on the road, two cars stop, but when the drivers see her face, they pull away before she can get in the car. Some laugh at her, some tell her she's going to hell for looking the way she does. Finally, a middle-aged man in a Mazda stops. He doesn't say much, but he offers her a can of Coke and a cheese sandwich from a cooler on the backseat. Mary falls asleep, and when she wakes up the man has stopped the car on the side of the road and is stroking her leg. She can't see his face, but his touch is gentle. When he sees she is awake, he stops what he's doing and starts the car. "It's okay," Mary tells him and pulls her tank top up over her head. His hand is warm and moist on her shoulders and neck, and her back. He caresses her, and at one point he presses his face to her back and breathes in deeply. When it's over, the man starts the car again and drives until they reach a truck stop. He drops Mary off there after handing her a twenty dollar bill and two more cans of Coke. Mary thanks him for his kindness.

Traveling Companions

The first person who joins her is a giant, and he finds her at a gas station in Lansing, Michigan where she is eating her lunch, and he has stopped to buy a pack of Camel Lights. When he says hello to her, she has to shield her eyes with her hand and look up, like she is trying to find a sparrow on a telephone line. He smiles and folds his body into itself so he can sit down next to her, and they talk until he has smoked all of his cigarettes.

In Milwaukee, Mary and the giant meet a man with tattoos of ghosts all over his body. He says they are the ghosts of all the people he has ever loved, and all the people he will love. Mary thinks the man will kill himself, but when she and the giant leave Milwaukee, he comes with them. They meet people in every city they come to, men with tattoos or missing limbs, giants, women with patterns of scars on their faces or muscles like men. They walk through Wisconsin, Iowa, Nebraska, Wyoming. Mary is proud of her friends, proud of the looks they get in cafes and shopping centers, on the sidewalks and streets. They have nowhere to go, nowhere they need to be, and so they walk with her.

Purpose

Finally, Mary tells them her plans. "I'm looking for Julia," she says, and they listen to her talk about Julia, about how she must be found. They like the idea of finding this woman who has been dead over a hundred years but whose body is hidden in the basement of a museum somewhere in Europe. They like the idea of bringing her home to Mary, of reuniting them. "We have to make money," Mary tells them, and so they decide to travel the country and work where they can, to save and be frugal. They are a practical group, and they want to help Mary all they can. They will help her all they can.

Second Love

The man with the ghosts has tattooed Mary's face on his chest, and he tells the giant that she won't leave him alone in his dreams. He says she lies next to him, warming him with her body, and he wakes up with the smell of animal on his clothes. The giant asks him what he thinks it means, and the tattooed man tells him he doesn't know, but he is falling in love with the smell. When the giant tells Mary what the tattooed man has said, she takes him aside, tries to reason with him, but he shows her the tattoo and she knows he can't be reasoned with. At night while the rest are sleeping, Mary slips away. She leaves a blanket covered in her fur at the tattooed man's feet and a note for the others saying not to look for her, she will return as soon as she can.

Family

There are six gorillas at the zoo—one huge black and silver one sitting on a flat red rock, and three smaller ones, two of them holding babies, walking around and preening each other. Mary can't stop staring at them. The really big one watches her for a while, and then comes over to where she is standing in front of the fence. He crouches there on all fours, knuckles in the dirt, with his head raised and his eyes directly on her. She knows if she waits long enough, he will talk to her. Any minute he'll open his mouth and speak. Pretty soon the others come up to crouch with him, and

Mary and the gorillas watch each other for a long time. She doesn't know how long. They seem so intelligent, so like people somehow, with their wrinkled hands that clasp each other, their faces, their small dark eyes.

Children

Mary gets a job at a library shelving books five hours a day. She doesn't talk to people, and sometimes she sits on the floor between the bookshelves and reads until she hears someone moving nearby, and then she jumps up and pushes the book cart down a row or two. She reads *Everything You Ever Wanted to Know About Sex, But Were Afraid to Ask* and makes notes in the margins.

One afternoon, when it's nearly time for story hour, the children's librarian gets sick. Mary watches her run to the bathroom, hears her gag and vomit into the toilet. She comes out wiping her mouth, and tells Mary that she'll have to fill in for her. "There shouldn't be too many kids today," she says, and hands Mary a large, glossy copy of *Little Red Riding Hood*. "Good luck." Mary can smell the barf on her breath.

The children begin to file into the library, and Mary sits down in the small chair in front of a large rug covered in brightly colored ABCs. She holds the book open and looks at the pictures, at Little Red Riding Hood's long blonde hair peeking out from under her hood, at the basket she clutches in a delicate pink fist. The wolf is large and gray with unkempt fur, and he leers at Red and bares his teeth menacingly.

When the children see Mary, some of them begin to cry. They run back to their parents and cling to their legs, say they want to go home. The braver ones stare at her and ask her why she looks so strange. "What are you?" they ask, and reach their hands toward her fur. "Be quiet," Mary tells them, opening the book to the first page, "it's time for the story." The children calm down as she begins to read to them, and by the end of the book they are staring at her with wide eyes. "And so the wolf ate Little Red Riding Hood up," Mary says, smiling at them, "and no one ever saw her again."

In the Library

(What really happens in the library is that the children's librarian throws up and then asks Mary to take over story time. "We're reading Little Red Riding Hood," she says, and hands Mary a large, bright copy of the book. "It's mostly pictures," she says, and smiles. "The kids love them." Mary sits in a chair in front of the ABC rug and reads to the children, who are polite and quiet. She growls like the wolf and says "Grandmother, why are your teeth so big" in a high, sweet voice, and the children stare at her, rapt. No one asks about her fur or says anything that could be considered rude in any way, but when she's finished with the book, they gather around her and try to sit in her lap. They put their arms around her neck and bury their faces in her chest and giggle when the fur tickles their noses. They look at her like she is beautiful, like she is something they are imagining instead of seeing.)

Story Hour

(The children's librarian throws up, but says she doesn't need to go home. She is pregnant, and is used to throwing up by now. She asks Mary to stand by in case she needs her, but that she can read the

all the red cars

story to the kids. "Little Red Riding Hood," she says, and smiles weakly. "My favorite. I always loved the wolf, even though my mom said that was weird." "I loved the grandmother," Mary says, and the children's librarian laughs. The children listen attentively to the story and cheer when Little Red Riding Hood pops out of the wolf's stomach, clean and neat, not a hair on her head harmed. Smiling.)

The Engagement

Lent has asked Julia to marry him, and she has accepted. He knelt down, took her hand in both of his, and told her he would be good to her. When she asked him if he loved her, he said of course he did. "I want to quit traveling," she told him, and he just smiled. "There's time to discuss that." She knew what he meant by this but said yes anyway, told him she would marry him in April when the trees were blooming. It was January then, and now it is nearly March. To save money, Julia is making her own wedding gown. Each night she works on it until her eyes swim, until she pricks herself with the needle and has to quit for fear of getting blood all over the satin. Lent doesn't mention the dress, or the flowers, or anything, only that he has a friend who will marry them for next to nothing. He wants the wedding to be sooner, the middle of March, but Julia tells him she won't be ready until late April. "Don't you want it to be perfect?" she asks him, and he says of course he does. She knows he is lying, but she smiles. "These things take time," she says, and goes back to her sewing.

Reunion

Mary stays away for months, and when she comes back they are all waiting for her, except the tattooed man is gone. The giant tells her he left the morning after Mary herself left, that he woke up and found the blanket, and they all watched him pack his things into his Army knapsack and walk away. He says the tattooed man didn't talk to anyone, and no one tried to stop him from leaving. Mary thinks about the tattooed man, but she doesn't talk about him with the rest of them. She wonders if he is safe, if he has kept the blanket or given it away.

The Book

"Here," the giant says, handing Mary a book, "I got this for you." On the cover is a woman standing with her legs wide apart and her hands on her hips. She is short, with very full lips and a broad, flat nose. She is covered in dark fur, has long tufts of it hanging from her chin and the sides of her face, but she wears a beautiful blue dress with flowers and birds embroidered all over it. It is low-cut, emphasizing her full breasts, and she wears a string of large pearls around her neck with a cross hanging from it. Her shoes are old-fashioned and high-heeled, with buttons and pointed toes. There are feathers and rhinestones in the woman's hair. Mary stares at the picture, running her finger over the woman's face. Julia.

The Book

(The giant never gives Mary the book. She already knows about everything in it. So he reads it over and over again, and when he begins to dream about Julia, he puts the book in his backpack and decides he won't look at it again until the dreams stop. But they don't.)

Ghosts

The next time Mary sees the tattooed man, it is in California. He is working at a small bar on the coast, and when Mary and the others walk in, he tells them he has known for days that they were coming. "I want to find Julia," Mary tells him, and tells him the story. He just nods at her. The only other person in the bar is a pale woman in a leather dress, and the bar smells like her perfume. The tattooed man says her name is Angela. Mary watches him watch her as she drinks beer from a tall glass.

They spend the night with the tattooed man in his studio apartment, and none of them sleep. The tattooed man keeps them awake telling stories about women and men he used to know, about the countries he has seen and the cities in those countries where he has lived. In the morning he makes scrambled eggs, pancakes with cherries and almonds, fresh juice, but Mary can't swallow a bite. When the tattooed man hugs her goodbye, he tells her she has gotten thin, that she is wasting away.

Stepmother

When Mary comes home for a visit, for the first time since she left, her father is living with a woman named Carla who irons his clothes every day and makes cheesecakes for dessert. He is happy, and when he hugs Mary she smells strong cologne. Carla stares at Mary for a minute before shaking her hand, and then uses both hands to grasp one of Mary's. "It is *so* nice to meet you." Carla has made salad, mashed potatoes, roast turkey served on a thick green glass platter she says was her grandmother's. She sits next to Mary's father and asks polite questions about Mary's friends, a boyfriend, a job. Mary talks about traveling, says nothing about men. She starts to tell them about Julia, but instead tells Carla that her grandmother had good taste in servingware. After dinner Carla stays in the kitchen running the dishwasher until bedtime.

Stepmother

(Mary's stepmother is short and dumpy, but she has a beautiful smile and wears shirts that show off her large, round breasts. Mary likes her. She smiles at Mary and gives her the largest slice of blackberry cheesecake on a pale green china plate. When it's time to clear the table Mary offers to wash the dishes, but Carla just laughs and says "Let me show you something." When they get into the kitchen, Carla motions toward the sink. Where there used to be just cabinets is a huge, silver dishwasher. "Straight out of a cooking show," Carla says. "Your dad bought it as a wedding gift."

"It's enormous," Mary says.

"It's top of the line," Carla replies, "the best there is. You can fit an entire five course meal's worth of dishes in there and you don't even have to rinse them first." Mary helps her load plates and bowls and silverware, and then Carla asks if she wants a drink. "Just one," she says, "because we worked so hard."

When her father comes into the kitchen to check on them, Mary and Carla are sitting at the table drinking whiskey and laughing. "You have a beautiful daughter," Carla tells him.)

Beauty

The giant is in love. He smiles when he talks about the girl, and his hands shake so much that Mary has to light his cigarettes for him. He says he doesn't know what to do with himself anymore, and Mary tells him she understands. Mary has never been in love, but she imagines it feels like trying to swallow your own tongue. They met the girl the giant is in love with in Wyoming. She is thin and blonde and wears worn jeans and a leather Stetson hat, and a large dog follows her everywhere. At night while she's sleeping, the giant hunches next to the girl, watches her until morning. If he reaches out to touch her, the dog growls softly.

Beauty

(The giant is in love with Mary, but he likes to watch the girl in the Stetson and imagine fucking her. She is blonde and small and tan but not dark, and her voice is soft. The giant watches the other men watching her, and tells himself he is in love.)

Traffic

Mary stays awake until nearly sunrise and listens to cars traveling down the highway. She can tell the colors of the cars based on their sound, and she makes note of how many of each color pass. She wonders why there are so many red ones. She watches the giant sleep, curled in his sleeping bag next to the beautiful girl in the Stetson, and feels her throat closing in on itself. It has been weeks since she began dreaming about him. Mary counts cars and awakening birds and the number of times the dog turns in its sleep, but by dawn she gives up. As she falls asleep she wonders where the red cars are going, if the men and women inside them have been driving all night just to get somewhere warm.

Traffic

(Mary hates the sound of cars passing on the interstate. There are just too many people in them, and their stories keep her from concentrating.)

Rooms

Sometimes they stay in hotels. When it rains or snows, when they don't want to fight bums for space on the sidewalks, when one of them has made some money, they get a room in a place along the highway and bunk down for the night. The girl in the Stetson loves hotel rooms and always takes a bed for herself, but Mary and the giant would prefer to sleep outside. They make a show of rolling their eyes at the girl in the Stetson when she gets excited about a Days Inn or Highway 81 Motor Lodge, but Mary is the only one who is really impatient. The giant grins at the girl when she pouts at

first love:
She can't see his face
but his touch is gentle

him and usually ends up sleeping next to her bed. The others don't care about sleeping, so they play on the furniture and flip channels on the TV all night. They always leave early in the morning before the housekeeper comes, two at a time so the desk clerk won't notice them. Before they go, Mary writes her name on a piece of paper and tucks it into the phonebook so anyone who finds it will know she's been there.

Correspondence

Mary writes letters to her sisters and mails them from mailboxes in neighborhoods she passes along her way. *Dear Lula*, she writes, *have you talked to Dad recently? Are you married yet?* And *Dear Mel, I passed a building on fire yesterday. The smell reminded me of you.* Her sisters never write her back, but Mary tells herself it's because she's always on the move and they can't find her. Sometimes she sends them packages—photographs of sidewalks and street vendors, postcards, bits of tree bark and ballpoint pens, and she always includes a card that says *Love, Mary.* Mary doesn't remember what her sisters look like, but she sees their faces in all the women she passes.

Correspondence

(Mary writes letters to her sisters and mails them from mailboxes in neighborhoods she passes along the way.

"Dear Mel," she writes,

"Do you remember when we were kids and you used to hold me on your lap? I was too big for you, but you always tried. Lula made fun of you for it, but you did it anyway, and I never thanked you.

I passed a burning building the other day and thought about our house, that stupid gas fire with the fake logs. I thought about you, how I'm not sure I'd recognize your face if I saw you, but I swear for just a second that every woman I pass is you. Give my love to Lula. Mary."

And
   "Dear Lula,
   I made this collage for you from notebook paper and magazine pictures. The girl in the middle (she is missing a head) is you. She's missing a heart, too, but you can't see it.
Love,
Mary")

The Fat Woman

In the South, Mary and her friends meet a fat woman. She says people call her Truck, but her name is Leanne. She is married, but it has been years since she and her husband lived together. "He can't stand the weight," she says, grasping the fat on her belly and shaking it a little. She reads the group his letters, and tells them she used to write back to every one, but now she doesn't even read them. She carries them in a small green suitcase that is so full she can barely close it. Mary tells her she should throw them away, perhaps even burn them, but she says she likes taking the old ones out sometimes and smelling them. "They smell like our house," she says, and holds one in front of Mary's face. Mary smells cigarette smoke, something sweet like bayberry. At night Truck cries in her sleep, and so Mary climbs into bed with her and holds her. The first night, she woke up immediately and told Mary to go away, to leave her alone, but now she just murmurs and pulls Mary's arm tighter around her body. Mary presses her face against Truck's back, feels the dampness of her skin, the fat underneath. She breathes in, tries to suck the skin into her nostrils, thinks about smothering herself with another person's flesh. When Truck asks her what she's doing, Mary doesn't answer.

Third Love

Truck tells the others that she and Mary are a couple, that she never thought she could be with a woman but there's something different about a woman covered in fur. She giggles and preens around Mary, says she hasn't felt this way in years, not since she and her husband first got together. "He wouldn't believe it if I told him," she says, "not me." The others don't say much, but Mary can tell they're curious. Mary isn't in love with Truck, but she enjoys the feel of her flesh. They hold hands sometimes, and Truck presses her legs against Mary's when they sit next to each other.

Truck leaves the door to the bathroom open when she showers, and when she gets out she shakes her head like a dog and sprays Mary with water. And when she eats, she chews her food exactly forty times before swallowing it. "It helps with digestion," she says. She has burned all the letters from her husband, and even the suitcase she kept them in. It smoldered and stank for days, and when it finally burned down, Truck danced barefoot in the ashes. All of these things make Mary think maybe she could love her, given enough time, but the dreams about the giant don't stop. In most of them he is large, larger even than in real life, and Mary feels surrounded by him. Sometimes he picks her up, and she can see over the tops of the trees and houses and everything looks tiny, like she is miles and miles away from it. He doesn't speak in the dreams, but Mary tells him everything she sees. In other dreams, he is the small one, and when she lifts him up he can balance on her shoulders like a dancer. He is light and lithe, and twirls on her shoulders, does pirouettes and handstands on her head. Truck thinks these dreams mean Mary needs to get away from the giant, that he is stifling her creativity, but Mary knows they mean something else.

Swamp

The group visits a cypress swamp. They walk on a bridge built over the water, and throw pebbles in to try to rouse alligators. The giant swears he sees nostrils poking up from the murk, but the others don't see anything. The sweat on their faces shines, and Mary's fur is heavy and damp. The cloud of mosquitoes humming around them is so thick that she worries about breathing them in every time she inhales. The girl in the Stetson stops to take photographs of everything, and Mary walks ahead. No one tries to catch up with her, but every once in a while they yell something, or whistle, or make some other noise to get her attention. She turns around and smiles at them, and keeps walking.

When the trail ends, Mary is far ahead of her friends, so she waits for them to catch up. She watches dragonflies skim the water, and when she turns her head, there is a turtle next to her, resting on a rotting log. When her friends finally reach her, the girl in the Stetson and the giant are holding hands. He dangles her camera by its strap from one of his fingers. Mary turns away and looks at the water. She hears gurgling and splashing sounds, sounds of something choking or calling its mate, but she doesn't know where they come from.

Swamp

(Mary meets Truck at the swamp, where she is sitting on a nearly rotten log next to a turtle that hisses when Mary and the others walk by. Truck doesn't talk, but shows Mary letters from her husband, letters in which he tells her she is too big for him. She nearly smothered him one night after they drank a bit too much, and he will not forget. Truck touches Mary's fur, says she has never seen anything like her, and Mary says she has never seen anything like Truck. And she hasn't.)

Purpose

("We're looking for Julia," Mary tells her friends, but she doesn't know what to say when they ask her what she wants to do with Julia when they find her. It will take a long time. Mary doesn't know where she is. Russia, maybe. Norway. She has told them they must be in it for the long haul. They smile at her, switch channels on the TV, rub their faces between the bed pillows. They tell her to lead the way.)

Bodies

The giant and the girl in the Stetson have started having sex—most of the time at night, and Mary tries to lie down as far away from them as she can, but during the day sometimes, too, when the group has stopped to have lunch or to rest. They hold hands and walk side by side away from the group, or the giant picks the girl up and carries her into the bushes. They come out a little while later with twigs and leaves in their hair, red faced and smiling. The other women in the group tease the girl in the Stetson, giggling like high school girls and asking her if the giant is giant all over. She blushes and scratches her dog's ears, and won't look anyone in the eye.

Mary can't help but hear them most nights, even though she knows they try to be quiet, and even though she sleeps with her pillow crushed against her ears—the giant gasps and groans, and the girl yelps softly. The dog sleeps next to Mary now, his back against hers. Sometimes Mary falls asleep to the sounds the giant and the girl make, and she dreams that they are two wolves killing each other, teeth tearing at throats and claws scraping flesh raw. When she wakes up, she has to walk over to where the two are sleeping and make sure they are still whole.

Limbs

It is past midnight, and Mary can't sleep. She listens to night sounds and tries to calm herself by stroking the fur on her legs and feet. She remembers petting herself like this when she was very young, playing with the fur in between her toes, and rubbing her calves and ankles with her feet, warming the fur. There is something about it that makes her feel safe. The others have been asleep for hours, it seems, but lately Mary has found sleeping more and more difficult. Most of the time she stays awake all night. She hugs Truck until she falls asleep, and then she slips out of bed, careful not to wake her. Sometimes she goes for walks, or reads, or just lies and waits until dawn.

Mary imagines what it would be like to see her mother, what they would say to each other, if they would hug, or shake hands, or simply stand side by side with their arms brushing against each other. She thinks about Julia, old and worn and musty, in a glass box with her baby perched beside her. She looks at herself in the mirror, at the fur covering her skin, and wonders if this is what Julia saw every time she saw herself, or if Julia saw an animal, a monster. Mary wonders why she can't help thinking of her mother every time she thinks about Julia. She imagines her mother exactly as she is in the photographs—tall, sturdy, with strong hands and thick eyebrows, long dark hair and pale skin. She clutches Mary's hand in hers and pulls her with her as she walks, so fast Mary's feet barely touch the ground.

Bodies

(The giant and the girl in the Stetson have started having sex, but every time they do it he can't stop wondering how different it would be with Mary. The girl in the Stetson has delicate bones, and he tells her he is afraid of crushing her, afraid of rubbing her tissue-thin skin raw. She laughs and climbs on top of him, says he is like a tree and she wants to wrap her legs all the way around him. She says she was a gymnast when she was younger, and has remained flexible. He watches her body as it moves on top of his and it is beautiful, though he wishes it had more substance.)

Feed

Mary and Truck lie in bed. Truck breaks a pomegranate open and

passes the seeds to Mary. Mary likes to feel them burst between her teeth. Truck braids the fur on Mary's arm, ties the braids with tiny rubber bands. They look out the window at trucks passing and crows picking at road kill. It is morning, and they haven't slept. "We should have breakfast," Truck says, and Mary pictures her eating eggs, the yolk on her chin, slurping the whites. She crushes a pomegranate seed between her fingers and the juice spurts onto the pillow next to Truck's head. "Watch it," Truck says. She gets up and pulls a thin cotton dress over her head, breathing heavily. The dress is tight on her gigantic thighs and hangs down past her ankles. She is short and round, her legs purple-red and strung with large veins. Her arms are muscular, and when she moves, the muscles flex and ripple under the layers of fat. The air conditioner blows icy air through the room, but her face is pink and sweaty. Mary watches her, afraid that at any moment she might have a heart attack or a stroke. If Truck falls across the bed, Mary will be smothered by her weight. Mary doesn't want to be cruel, but she knows it's true. "Why don't you get up?" Truck says, standing at the mirror and combing her hair. "We should go out." Mary turns on the television and watches morning cartoons.

The Show

Lent is touching her again, his hand on her arm, grasping her elbow. He thinks if he touches her, the audience will think he cares, will think he is protecting his wife. Julia shrugs him off, stands with her hands on her hips, looks out into the crowd. "I dare you," she wants to say, but instead she smiles, gives them a wink. The pearls roped around her neck are fake, but she made her dress herself, embroidered every last flower while Lent was out doing God knows what. He comes home at night stumbling, but they sleep in separate beds so he doesn't wake Julia up. She sleeps soundly, always has, and she is grateful. Lent can stomp down the hall in heavy boots, can knock over chairs and birdcages on his way to bed, and she won't hear him.

She cleans up after him the next morning and can't help fantasizing about him falling one night, striking his head on the edge of the heavy oak table. What if she walked into the dining room one morning, on the way to make breakfast, and there he was—collapsed on the floor, not breathing, perhaps already cold? Julia can hardly bear to think about it. Her palms begin to sweat, and she feels her face flush under her fur. Sometimes she smiles to herself without knowing it, and Lent asks her what she's thinking. "I'm thinking about the show," she tells him, "my next number. The dress I'm making." And she lifts up the yellow satin to show him, holds it up to herself, but he has already stopped listening. He nods, tells her he'll be back in a while, and Julia goes back to her sewing. When he comes home, his clothes smell like perfume—the kind prostitutes wear, cheap and flowery—but Julia washes them in harsh detergents that take the smell away.

Possibilities

Los Angeles, Boston, New York City, Minneapolis, Atlanta. Rome. Prague. London. Museum of Curiosities (she isn't a curiosity). Moscow. Closer. Closer. The U.S. is out. Mary has known this for quite some time, though she spoke with a woman who thought Julia may have been brought to Chicago for a World's Fair exhibition in the early 1900s and left there. Reykjavik. Helsinki. Closer still. Mary's eyes are blurry from staring at the computer screen. She can't afford to travel very far in Europe, so she makes phone calls, surfs the internet. "You should have been doing this all along," Truck says.

"I was," Mary tells her. "But everyone wanted to travel, so we did. There wasn't any hurry before." The others are gone, have dropped away quietly one by one until the only people left in the group are Mary, Truck, the giant, and the girl in the Stetson. And they are tired of traveling.

"Why's there a hurry now?" Truck asks, and Mary shrugs.

"Maybe there isn't one," she says, "but it's time."

Correspondence—Dead Letter

Dear Mary,

I know you probably don't want to hear from me (I wouldn't if I were you), but I've been looking for you for a long time now. Your father told me you move around a lot, so I hope this gets to you. I think of you often, all the time, and I wonder how you are. There is a lot to say, but I don't even know if you'll get this, so I'll wait to hear back from you before I say any more. If you don't want to write back, I understand. But I hope you will.

Love,
Mom

p.s. Here is a photograph I took in Hawaii of a volcano just starting to erupt. It reminds me of you.

Correspondence—Dead Letter

Dear Mary,

You must not be getting my letters, or else you don't want to hear from me. I hope it's not the latter. I wish I could sit down with you and explain why I left—I just can't write it in a letter. I've tried, and it always comes out sounding so stupid. What I *can* say is this: I wanted to take you with me and have always regretted not doing it. I thought about coming back so many times, just to get you. You would have been unhappy, though, at least this is what I tell myself. I've moved around a lot—all over the country, and even to Scotland for a few years, and then to Canada. I think my next stop might be South Africa. I think there's a country song that says something like "I wasn't born for settling down," and it's a cliché but in my case it's true. It sounds like it might be true for you, too. I don't regret marrying your father and having kids, but I wish I had done some traveling first. Might have made it easier on everyone. If you get this, please write back, even if it's just to tell me to piss off.

Love,
Mom

p.s. Sometimes I do regret having Lula.

Correspondence—Dead Letter

Dear Mary,

I wish you would come home. It's boring here and I can't torment Mel and Dad the way I liked to torment you. It just isn't the same. Where are you these days? Have you joined the circus yet?

Love,
Lula

The Husband

Truck has gotten a stack of letters from her husband telling her he wants her back. He has included photographs of himself which show the weight he's gained, a hundred pounds, he says, and he tells her he gained it out of sympathy for her. "Our bodies will make sense together now," he says. He tells her he misses her, that he can't sleep at night because he thinks about her so much, and he needs her to come home. "The dog howls all the time," he says. "She only stops when I show her a picture of you." Mary can tell Truck is thinking about going, and she tries not to influence her one way or another. The letters keep coming, and at night when she thinks Mary is asleep, Truck unfolds them and kisses them. Sometimes she rubs her body with them, crinkling the paper over her breasts and stomach. Mary pretends to sleep, but she watches through half-closed eyes and knows it's only a matter of time before Truck leaves.

When she does, it is early morning, before the sun is up, and she packs quietly. She leaves one of her dresses in the closet and a small red stone for Mary. Mary keeps the stone in her pocket and wears the dress as a nightgown for weeks after. In the mornings, she finds it crumpled at the foot of the bed or stuck in the crack between the bed and the wall. She writes letters to Truck telling her she hopes her husband stays fat, but she doesn't send them.

The Husband

(Truck knows Mary's in love with the giant, and so when her husband starts asking her to come home again, she knows it's probably best. Everything he tells her is stuff he's seen in movies, but she likes the idea that he has remembered it well enough to say it to her.)

The Husband

(The giant is happy when Truck goes back to her husband. He tells the girl in the Stetson that he knew all along that it wouldn't work out. The girl in the Stetson just nods and shrugs. "I thought they were cute together," she says.)

The Husband

(The giant is happy when Truck leaves Mary to go back to her husband. He immediately breaks it off with the girl in the Stetson, who has known it was coming and has prepared herself. She tells the giant she's wanted to leave him for a long time, that she didn't want to hurt him, but she can't take it anymore. "We don't even have sex anymore," she says, "I think you might have a problem." After she's gone, he finds Mary and tells her what has happened. "I did it because I want to be with you," he says, but she tells him she needs to be alone. Since Truck left, she has been working all day and night because she can't sleep. She thinks she has found Julia, but she doesn't want to say anything until she is sure. "Don't tell me that fat woman broke your heart," he says. "Don't tell me that.")

Conception

Julia is pregnant. She can hardly believe it, and she starts to cry every time she thinks about it. Lent is excited too. He doesn't talk about it very much, but he doesn't stay out as often at night, and when he does come home late he doesn't smell like perfume. Julia has realized that she doesn't care if Lent loves her. She thought she did for a long time (perhaps when she believed he actually did *love her), but now when she thinks about it, she understands that it doesn't really matter at all. She is going to have a child—a little boy, she hopes, who will love her and be loved by her, and will grow up to be intelligent and will make his way in the world. She will not allow Lent to make a show of him, to parade him around in front of people who gasp and laugh and talk about him like he isn't even in the room. The chances of the child looking like Julia must be slim, she thinks, and so it probably won't even be an issue. But if he is, God forbid it, she is going to insist that he not be put on display like she has been. She hasn't minded it, really. She has gotten to see the world, and has made plenty of money. Though they don't always show it, people respect her. They are amazed that someone can look like her and still be intelligent and cultured, and Julia is. But she wonders what it would be like to have a normal life—a house full of children, the only traveling being trips to the seashore in summertime. A husband who doesn't come home smelling like other women. When the baby is born, this is what Julia will insist on. They have traveled enough, have made enough money to sustain them for quite some time. Lent has always talked about writing a book, and Julia can give singing lessons for something to do. When it is nearly time for the baby to be born, Julia will tell Lent to announce her retirement. It is the least he can do for her.*

Fourth Love

A few weeks after Truck and the girl in the Stetson leave, Mary and the giant end up sleeping together, and then they are together every day. They move into an apartment, and then rent a house in a small town in Indiana where the giant used to have family. It happens so quickly, and Mary didn't expect it (she still thinks about Truck's heavy legs wrapped around her own and the way she smells, her breath), but she is happy. They drink wine in bed, and he tells her she is more beautiful than any woman he's seen. "You're an idiot," Mary tells him, but he swears it's true.

The giant is neither too heavy nor too light on her body, and she loves the way her fur feels against his skin, almost like it is absorbing him. She tries to tell the giant this, but he doesn't understand. "It doesn't matter," she says. They whisper "I love you" to each other over and over until Mary doesn't know what the words mean anymore; she just likes the sounds and the way they feel on her tongue.

fur:
A coating similar to the
pelt of a mammal

3: HOME

Flight

It is time. Mary has been in contact with the curator of a museum in Norway, and Julia is there. When she tells the giant she's found her, he kisses her and says "of course you have" like he always believed she would. They makes plane reservations for the trip to Oslo, and the giant says it can be their honeymoon, but Mary isn't listening to him. Her body feels heavy now, and all she wants to do is sleep. She's found Julia. She could have found her months ago, but she is almost glad she waited so long. Now that the time has finally come, she is terrified. What will she do with her? Why did she want her so badly in the first place? *You're traveling to Norway to bring a dead body home with you,* she says to herself. She has never thought about how strange of an idea it is, and now that she does, it seems impossibly strange. The giant books first class tickets, a suite in the Grand Hotel. "This is the first time we'll really get to be alone together," he says. Mary is sitting on the bed, and he jumps on it and drops down next to her. "Aren't you excited?"

"Yes, but we really won't be alone together," Mary says. "We'll have Julia with us."

Bright Houses

Oslo is a city of brightly painted houses. Electric blues and reds and yellows. They look like they've been colored with crayons. Most of them are strung with Christmas lights, even though Christmas isn't for months yet. The city is so dark, their cabdriver says, that people are obsessed with light. They burn candles in their houses all the time, cover every open surface with lamps. "Every once in a while, we get a letter from the public works saying we need to cool it with using so much electricity," he says, "but no one listens." The giant takes photograph after photograph of the houses, of all the buildings they pass. He thinks they're beautiful, but Mary thinks the city is tacky, like a miniature city in a toy train set. "It's like it's trying to be beautiful," she says, but she feels bad after saying it. The giant just frowns and takes more pictures. Most of them turn out badly, just smears of colored light and indeterminate shapes, but Mary loves them. She can't take her eyes off of them. "This is the real city," she says, "you've captured it."

Bright Houses

(The giant loves Oslo. He asks Mary how she would feel about moving there one day, and shows her photographs he took in the cab and on the train. The houses are painted bright blue and red and yellow, and they have Christmas lights strung over their windows and eaves, even though Christmas is still months away. The photographs come out badly—just smears of red and green and pink light over shadow—but Mary says they're beautiful. She tells the giant that when they get home she is going to print them out and frame them. She wants to hang them in Julia's room.)

City of Bright Houses

(The citizens of Oslo are obsessed with light. They burn candles in their windows and keep Christmas lights hanging from their roofs even in summer. Most of the streetlights are always burning, even in the morning and afternoon. "It is because there is so little natural light," the cab driver tells Mary. "Most of us suffer from vitamin D deficiencies because the city is so dark." Mary tells him he should take vitamins, and he pulls a bottle out of the glovebox and shakes them at her. "Every day," he says.)

Julia

And there she is. She looks more like a stuffed animal, one of those cheap giant bears you get at a state fair, than something that was once alive. She could be a toy left in the attic after the owner grew up and moved away from home. Her dress is brown with age and dust, and the hair covering her body is matted and dirty. It has fallen—or been pulled—out in clumps, and the skin underneath is dark gray and leathery. She is missing an arm. "She looks like a dust mop," the giant says, and Mary tells him to shut up. "Where's her baby?" she asks, and the man from the museum points to a small thing in the corner. There is nothing about the child that looks human, except for its limbs. They're straight and slender, and the child stands on a tall iron perch like a bird. "That stand isn't the original. It's supposed to be wood," Mary says. "No," the man from the museum says, "we never found the original. This is as close as we could get." Mary moves closer to Julia and puts a hand on her dress. "She needs to be cleaned." "Yes," says the man. "We really haven't known what to do with her." "It's good I found you when I did," Mary says, "you people would have just let her rot." The man looks like he wants to say something, but doesn't.

They load Julia and the baby into the van, wrapping them in blankets before laying them down on the seats. Julia takes up an entire row of seats by herself, and they lay the baby on top of her, buckling them in so they won't slide around. The bodies smell musty, like very old library books, and Mary breathes in deeply. She turns around every few seconds to look at Julia, imagining her face under the faded blue blanket covering it, her glass eyes scratched and dull. "What do you think she looked like when she had just died? When she was first preserved?" the giant asks Mary, putting a hand on her shoulder. "They've made such a mess of her it's hard to tell what she was like before." "She was beautiful," Mary says. "Look at the pictures."

Customs

They have a letter from the museum, and one from the American embassy, and these are the only things that help them get Julia and her son through customs. The customs agents threaten to cut Julia open, to make sure Mary and the giant aren't smuggling drugs, but they talk to the museum director on the phone and he convinces them not to do it. "You're lucky," one of the agents tells Mary. They pack Julia and her son in bubble wrap and yards of tissue paper, and finally let them go to be loaded into the cargo area of the plane. "Be careful with her," the giant tells them, slipping one a 500 kroner note. The agent frowns at him, but puts the money in his pocket.

Home

In the guestroom, now Julia and the baby's room, Mary removes Julia's dress and begins to clean her. She is careful, very, but even so the dress crumbles in her hands. She drops the fabric to the floor, and it lies crumpled around Julia's feet. The giant watches Mary as she combs Julia's hair, gently tugging through the mats and spraying her lightly with perfume. "I'm going to have to make her a new dress," she says. "Can you sew?" He asks, but Mary doesn't answer. She combs and brushes Julia's fur until it is soft and fluffy, until it is hard to see the bald patches, and then cleans her face and eyes with a damp cloth. "She's looking a lot better already," the giant says as he leaves the room. Mary brushes every inch of hair on Julia's body and sneezes from the dust she stirs up. When she gets to Julia's feet, she washes them with the cloth. When she is done, she wraps Julia in the blue blanket again, folding and tucking it into a kind of sari. She hangs a string of plastic pearls around her neck. "Look at you," she says to Julia.

Family

The first few nights with Julia, Mary sleeps on the couch in the guestroom. "I want to be near them," she tells the giant, and most mornings she wakes up with him on a blanket on the floor next to her. Mary orders a new dress for Julia and clothes for the baby, and when the clothes arrive she dresses them carefully. She and the giant take photographs with them, and then photographs of the two by themselves. In one of the photographs, Mary is standing next to Julia with her hand resting gently on Julia's shoulder. They are both looking directly into the camera, and neither is smiling but they both look content. "Like mother, like daughter," Mary says when she sees it.

Fur

It's falling out. When she wakes up in the morning, it's all over the sheets. She showers, and it collects on the soap, in the drain. She can even pull it out in clumps, though it hurts a little. It is thinner and lighter, and when she goes to the doctor, the nurse congratulates her. "See?" she says, smiling and running a pink fingernail down Mary's arm, "this is just proof you should never give up hope." Mary looks at the fingernail and shrugs. "I was okay with it," she says, but the nurse isn't listening. She chews gum, rolling it from cheek to cheek with her tongue. "Dr. Mark will be right with you," she says.
The doctor examines Mary for two minutes, maybe less. "It's definitely coming out," he says, and Mary nods. "If you start to feel ill, or experience any other changes, call me. But it's probably just a hormone shift. There's no reason to think it won't all just come out on its own pretty soon and then you can just get on with your life."
    "I've been getting on with my life for years," Mary says. She puts on her shirt and leaves the doctor's office.

Fur

(It's falling out. Mary doesn't know what to do, and so she goes to the doctor. The giant drives her there. The doctor examines her, takes a skin scraping and a blood sample. "You're fine," he says, looking into her eyes and ears. "Most people with your condition find that the hair falls out eventually. It's usually in childhood, but you must be a late bloomer. It's just hormones, and they should regulate themselves after a little while." He smiles at her, his teeth flashing in the sterile light of the exam room.

"It's fur," Mary says under her breath.

"Excuse me?" the doctor says, the smile still on his face. He cocks his head as he tries to hear her better.

"Nothing," Mary says, and when he tells her to come back in three weeks so he can see her progress, she nods.)

Fur

(Every morning it's the same. Mary showers and then has to clean out the tub. She wipes clumps of dark fur out with paper towels, throws them in the trash. Sometimes she uses just her fingers, and holds the fur in her hands. It is heavy and soft and warm, like a living thing. She thinks she can feel it move. The giant comes in and finds her crying, and he tells her he isn't sure what to say, but it will be all right. Mary thinks he's secretly glad she's losing the fur, but then she tells herself that this is impossible. He buys her candy, and one day he comes home with flowers. She lets him put them in a vase next to the bed, but when he's not looking, she pulls the bud off one of the roses and crushes it between her fingers. She sleeps in the guestroom every night now, and the giant sleeps in their bed.)

Fur

(Fur: 1. The thick coat of soft hair covering the skin of a mammal, such as a fox or beaver.

2. The hair-covered, dressed pelt of such a mammal, used in the making of garments and as trimming or decoration.
3. A garment made of or lined with the dressed pelt of a mammal.
4. A coating similar to the pelt of a mammal.)

Confinement

It is nearly time for the baby to be born, and Julia cannot leave her bed. The doctor is worried about her. He says she has not carried the child well, and he is concerned that the birth will be complicated. Lent has been acting like the ideal husband. He brings her cups of chocolate and tea, peels oranges and feeds them to her like she is a child herself. When she asks him about retirement, he tells her she can do whatever she wants to do—it is her decision to make. "You just have this baby and get well, and then tell me what you want," he says, and leans down and kisses her forehead tenderly. Julia wonders why he is being so kind. She isn't sure she should trust Lent, but she is grateful. His company makes the confinement easier. She tells the nurses of her fears, but says she can't believe that her husband would betray her in that way. "Besides," she says, smiling, "he can't force me to work against my will, can he?"

Bare

When the fur is all gone, Mary takes photograph after photograph of herself and lays them all out on the bed side by side. She tries to smile in a couple of the photographs, but in most of them she is not. The woman in the pictures is small and pale, and she looks frightened, like she is going to disappear. When the giant comes home, Mary is in bed, or sometimes she is in the living room taping

peels oranges &
feeds them to

up the photographs. "Look at me," she says, "can you believe it?" The giant shakes his head, then takes off his shoes and curls up next to her in bed, or if she is not in bed, he comes up behind her and wraps his arms around her, pressing them into her belly. "It's different touching you now," he says, "a little scary, even." He smiles when he says this and seems nervous.

"Why scary?" Mary asks. She pulls away from him.

The giant moves toward her again, and puts his hands lightly on her waist. "Not scary," he says quickly, "not in a bad way. Just strange."

"I don't mind if it's scary," Mary says. "I just want to know why."

"It isn't, though," the giant says. "I was just being silly."

At night, next to him, Mary positions her body so that their arms are directly side by side. She tells the giant not to move, and he doesn't. In the dark, with only the light from the streetlamps outside coming in through the windows, their skin looks exactly the same. There is no difference between them.

Skin

Mary is cold all the time. She is normal now like everyone else, and to her this means she is cold and unrecognizable. She still jumps when she sees herself in the mirror, still can't believe that this is what she is now. The giant buys her sweaters and a new fluffy bathrobe. He says she needs to try harder to keep herself warm.

Skin

(Mary is cold all the time. She shuts all the windows and turns the heat up to 85, wears the giant's heavy wool socks and thick sweaters and stays huddled on the couch under a blanket all day. The giant laughs at her, tells her that non-furred people have been dealing with the cold for centuries now, this is nothing new, but Mary says it is new to her. He bundles her up in a heavy winter coat and a knit hat and mittens and makes her go for walks with him. It is only the beginning of October, and it is chilly, but not cold yet, and the people they pass look at Mary strangely. Some laugh at her, tell her to wait until December if she wants cold. "Cold is what I *don't* want," she tells them, but they don't pay any attention.)

Skin

(Mary is cold all the time, and worse, she doesn't recognize herself anymore. She is still short and squat, with thick limbs and strong muscles, she still has long dark hair on her head and blue eyes, slightly crooked teeth, but this is where the familiar ends. Her skin is whiter than any she has ever seen. Her fur was always too dense to allow much sun to get through, and now that it's gone, she looks like a pale, blind fish you might find at the bottom of the ocean. She is practically translucent. "I am a fish," she tells the giant, and puffs out her furless cheeks, purses her lips. "I live at the bottom of the dark ocean." And then she makes her face look normal again and shrugs. "I don't know what to do with myself anymore." The giant smiles at her and gives her sunscreen, tells her to rub it deep into her skin.)

Faces

Julia is dying. The doctors have done everything they can for her, but the bleeding will not stop. She hears them say that her body couldn't handle the birth, that the baby tore up her insides. She wants to tell the baby she forgives it. The curtains around her bed block out the light from the windows, and she lies in darkness wishing she could sleep and wishing she didn't feel so cold. She wants to hold her baby, but the nurse won't let her. Lent is outside. When she finally sleeps, she dreams about her home. The dirt there, dry and powdery like sand, the trees with shallow roots and long spiny branches that give no shade, the sky bright with sun. She has not seen it since she was a baby, but in her dream it is as clear as if she were still there. She opens her mouth and she is speaking Spanish to a woman in a brown dress. Her mother. Her mother puts her hand on Julia's face, stroking the soft fur on her cheek and welcoming her home.

How

Mary wonders how she got here. When she asks the giant, he just shrugs and smiles. "I ask myself the same thing all the time."

Mary swats him, and says "Come on. I'm serious."

"Seriously," he says, "I do." "What are we?" she asks him, running her hands through her hair until it stands on end. "How did we become this?"

"I really don't know," he says, "I'd tell you if I did." She hasn't told the giant yet, but Mary is going to have a baby. She wonders if this is why she lost the fur, if there has been some sort of hormonal shift. The doctor says it is possible, but he would have to run more tests to be sure. Mary wonders how she got to this place—she can now walk through the aisles of the grocery store without people staring, can go anywhere she wants and be invisible. Now she is invisible.

Mary goes into the room where they keep Julia and her son. She brushes Julia gently with a soft brush, straightens her dress and the strand of pearls around her neck. She runs her hand down Julia's arm, rubs pieces of the coarse fur between her fingers. She doesn't look at Julia's face. She pretends it isn't there.

Help

They hear peacocks and monkeys all day and all night. The peacocks' cries are like those of small children, and Mary runs outside thinking someone is in trouble, one of the neighbor's girls has been hurt riding her bike or roller skating and needs help. That's what the peacocks seem to be saying: *Help.* Mary stands in the middle of the yard and looks around. The grass is covered by orange and brown leaves, and the trees are almost completely bare. The nights and mornings are cold, and Mary swears she can smell snow in the air, but the giant says she's crazy. "It's not even November yet," he says. When Mary comes back inside, he's laughing. "It's going to take you a while, huh?" He kisses her on the neck, near where her shoulder begins, and breathes in her smell. "Love you," he says, and Mary smiles at him. She puts away groceries and cleans the kitchen, says the word *Help* to herself, over and over again.

The Show

Julia and the boy are dead, and Lent is completely broke. There are gambling debts to pay, and then the rent with whatever is left over from that. He is pleased with himself for making sure his wife died ignorant of the state of their finances, but this doesn't stop him from worrying about where the money is going to come from. The whores he spends his nights with tell him to just start another sideshow, to find some more freaks to display, but Lent knows the age of sideshows is nearly over. Besides, no other freak he has dealt with has brought in the money that Julia did. This is as close to mourning his dead wife as Lent will get, though he tears up whenever someone mentions her name. Everyone knows he has been a good husband, loving Julia for her own sake.

He is at the undertaker's when it finally hits him, and he hopes it isn't too late. "I will pay you whatever it takes to keep her exactly as she is," Lent tells the undertaker, and claps his hands, "exactly as she is. I want them to recognize her when I bring her onstage and to expect her to start dancing just like she used to. Surely you can preserve her—you do it all the time."

"You're not going to bury her?" the undertaker asks.

"I'm going to take her with me wherever I go," Lent says, and now he's smiling. "It'll be just like it used to be. And I'll pay you extra if you can do the same for the boy. The crowd will love to see mother and child together."

"Let me see what I can do," the undertaker says. He is nervous about acting against propriety, and surely this is, but he has mouths to feed as well. He decides there can be no harm in it. He and his two assistants work day and night on Julia, removing her organs and pumping her full of spirits and wax, stuffing her body with linen. They can almost imagine what the Egyptians felt as they were preparing Tutankhamen for his sarcophagus, though he was a pharaoh and not a strange woman who had a face like a monkey and the fur to match. Finally, she is finished. The last parts they remove are her eyes, and they replace them with shiny black marbles. The real eyes roll around in a shallow metal pan until they are thrown into the gutter with the rest of the waste. They do the same for the deformed baby, and place him, standing upright, on a tall wooden perch.

"He looks like a damned parrot," Lent says when he sees the boy, but the more he looks at him, the more he likes him. Julia stands in a wide-legged stance, with her hands on her hips. The undertaker and his assistants have put her in her favorite dress, and have laced strands of pearls through her hair. She is wearing a pearl cross necklace that Lent brought her from South America when they were first married. Lent looks at her a long time, walking around so he can see her from different angles. At one point he puts a hand on her arm and strokes her fur, but he pulls it back almost immediately with a look of disgust on his face. He stares at her, walking around and around her, for nearly ten minutes straight without saying a word. "Fantastic," he finally breathes, straightening Julia's necklace, and he is too overwhelmed to say anything else. He takes the undertaker and his assistants out for a fine dinner to thank them for their brilliant work, and to celebrate the good fortune he feels sure is coming his way.

Correspondence

Dear Mom,

We have a small yellow house with a yard that needs cutting and five bird feeders in the front. You can't miss it. Here is a photograph of me. Without the fur (it fell out) I look a lot like you, only shorter. I wish I were tall like you. I'm going to have a baby. It's due in six months. Will you come to see it? I hope it's a girl, and I hope it looks like me.

Love,
Mary

Correspondence

Dear Mom,

It is cold all the time, and sometimes I'm scared. Sometimes I think I understand now, but you still shouldn't have left.

Love,

Mary

Lent and Julia

She watches him constantly. Every time he brings her out on stage, she stares at him until he feels the skin on the back of his neck start to get cold. He has tried standing beside her instead of in front of her, but he swears her glass eyes follow him wherever he goes. He can't sleep unless he drinks whiskey, and he has started finishing a bottle each night and then waking up drunk and sick at dawn. He covers her and the baby with sheets at night so he won't wake up to their eyes on him, but he knows she is watching him through her shroud. The undertaker who worked to preserve her refuses to have anything to do with Lent, and tells him he should have buried her properly in the first place. "You get what's coming to you," he says, and shuts the door in Lent's face.

Lent even thinks about Julia when he is with his whores—with blonde Janie whose nipples are pink and sweet as candy, even with his favorite, Sunny, who has always been able to make him forget whatever she doesn't want him to think about just by whispering in his ear. He'll be lying next to one of them, or both if he feels up to spending the money and time, and then he'll see Julia—standing in the corner with her hands on her hips, staring at him until he starts to scream. Those eyes. He knows they're not real, but they watch him. He can't make a move without them following him. The girls say he's crazy. They tell him his conscience is finally catching up to him, that he married that poor ugly woman and made her think he loved her, and now she's making him pay for it. They say he drinks too much, and they scold him and then pull his head down into their breasts and comfort him like he's a child. Lent thinks he is becoming a child. He needs Sunny and Janie to care for him, to protect him, and he spends every night he can with them until the madam tells him he needs to make room for better paying customers and forces him to leave. And when he is no longer allowed in their rooms, when even his Sunny and Janie refuse to see him, he goes to the pubs until closing and then locks himself in his office with a bottle of whiskey.

One night he is coming home, not as drunk as he had hoped to be, but certainly drunk, enough to be laughed at by the night watchman on the street as he staggers by. He has whiskey waiting for him, and he moves as quickly as he can to get to it. When he unlocks the door and enters the hall, there she is. Standing in a place he knows he did not leave her, staring him down. Lent can't take his eyes off of her—the cold glass mesmerizes him, and while he wants to look away, to turn and run as far away from her as his legs will take him, it is impossible. He begins to move toward her.

No one finds him for days, until finally his landlady comes into his rooms to clean. Lent is lying on the floor, his head gashed open, drying blood sticky on the floor all around him. His mouth is open, as if in surprise or shock, and he is stiff and cold.

"Must have tripped on this rug here," the policeman called to the scene says, "a terrible accident," and everyone at the inquest agrees.

Nualli

A woman in a small house in Indiana thinks about giving birth to a child covered in fur. She stays awake at night with her hands on her belly, remembering what it was like when *she* had fur, when she was covered in the same thick coat that animals are and was never cold. She thinks about her mother and sisters, and wonders if she will ever see them again. When she calls her father to tell him the news, that her daughter will be born in six months, he asks her to bring the baby home with her for a visit after she is born. She tells him she will try, but she is worried about how busy she will be. "Maybe you can visit us here," she says, and her father says he would like to do that.

Mary goes into Julia's room with the giant, and they sit on the couch talking about the baby. "It's all happened too fast," Mary says, and she wonders if they will stay together after the baby is born, or if she, like her mother, will give herself no choice but to leave. The giant knows what she's thinking, and he puts his arms around her and holds her tight. "You can't go," he says, "please don't think about it." But she does think about it, she can't help it. She wonders what will happen if the night finally comes when she knows it is no use to stay there, when she has to pack the car and leave only photographs behind. If she thinks about it long enough, she can actually picture it happening. It is late, the giant and the children are asleep, and she realizes she is done. She has to go, even though she doesn't know where. She knows she'll figure it out. She looks down at her sleeping daughter—the oldest this time, not the youngest—and touches the fur on her cheek gently. No matter how worried she is, she knows she has to take her daughter with her this time, that she will take her no matter what, so she does.

Women Born with Fur

A woman gives birth to a baby girl covered in fur—her face, her neck and body, everywhere. The only parts of her body that aren't furry are her palms and the soles of her feet. The woman crouches against a tree and sobs, is certain the gods have cursed her. The little girl squirms against her mother's chest and looks up, her eyes wide and dark. She tries to nurse, and at first her mother slaps her away, puts her roughly on the ground next to the tree. The baby doesn't even cry, and her mother picks her up again. After she has eaten, the baby falls asleep. Her mother wraps her in a wool blanket and some leaves, and lays her back down on the ground. When the morning comes they will find another place—a cave near the river, or somewhere in the mountains. The woman can hunt for food, can at the very least collect plants. No one will take them in, she knows, but she thinks they can take care of themselves.

ACKNOWLEDGEMENTS

Excerpts from *Women Born with Fur* can be found in *Thirty Under Thirty: An Anthology of Younger Writers*, edited by Lily Hoang and Blake Butler, and in *Map Literary: A Journal of Contemporary Literature* Vol. 2, Fall 2012.

ABOUT THE AUTHOR

Beth Couture received her Ph.D. in Creative Writing from the Center Center for Writers at the University of Southern Mississippi, MFA from the University of Notre Dame, MA from SUNY-Binghamton, and her Bachelor's from Hollins University. Her fiction has appeared in *Gargoyle*, *The Southeast Review*, *The Georgetown Review*, *Drunken Boat*, *The Yalobusha Review*, *Ragazine*, and in the anthology, *Thirty Under Thirty*. She currently lives in Philadelphia and is pursuing a Master's degree in Social Work at Bryn Mawr College.

ABOUT THE ARTIST

Rachel May is a writer and teacher who lives in New England. Her book, *Quilting with a Modern Slant*, was published in January 2014 and named a "Best Book of 2014" by *Library Journal* and Amazon.com (in two categories). The book has been favorably reviewed in *The Chicago Tribune, Publisher's Weekly, The Library Journal* (starred), *The Los Angeles Times, The Providence Journal*, and *MarthaStewartLiving.com*. In addition to her work in *Women Born with Fur* and *Out from the Pleiades*, a book of sewn images and fiction is forthcoming from Dusie Press in March 2015. She's recently finished a novel and is at work on a research project focusing on a quilt made between 1830 and 1950. Her writing has been twice nominated for the Pushcart Prize, won several awards and been noted in over a dozen contests. Work has recently appeared or is forthcoming in *Michigan Quarterly Review (and featured as cover image), New Delta Review, Cream City Review, Word for / Word, Indiana Review, The Literary Review, Green Mountains Review*, and other journals. She's been a resident and fellow at The Vermont Studio Center and The Millay Colony.

OUT FROM THE PLEIADES

A PICARESQUE NOVELLA IN VERSE

LESLIE McGRATH

Jaded Ibis Press
sustainable literature by digital means™
an imprint of Jaded Ibis Productions
Seattle • Hong Kong • Boston

"All cruelty springs from weakness."
—Seneca

"Let a man get up and say, Behold, this is the truth,
and instantly I see a sandy cat filching a piece of
fish in the background. Look, you have forgotten
the cat, I say."
–Virginia Woolf

We Come upon Mina

The crowded mountains she's driven down
                    jaggedly down
like a crack in porcelain
                            now seem a huddle
                    of distant cattle.

            The road jigged right
                    at a white clapboard church
& once she passed over
                    the temporary bridge
        that every car knocks the wind out of
                    she found a mill   (old wood, new paint)
                            & parked.

Here   Mina in her black down coat
                    down to the tops
                of her small black boots
    stood smoking
        cigarette after cigarette
                            lighting one
                        from the other

        furiously   furiously   furious.

                    College was turning out
                    to be a monumental bore
                    & the exercise of free speech
                    was often a bust.

Mina— born at the lip of a bullhorn
& at the tail
of a political age
was taught to speak her mind & speak it loudly

she raised her voice
more often than most students raise their hands
more often than parishioners raise their hearts.

Get out of Afghanistan, Imperialist pawns!

This she hissed at a counterful of soldiers
breakfasting at a dingy diner
near Westover Air Force base.

With a swiftness she hadn't counted on
one rushed at her full-on,
the top of his head hitting Mina's solar plexus
like a battering ram at a drum skin.

Bent like a pin, she fell
into the arms of another uniform
—a woman with uncommon
golden eyes—
who spun her toward the door, rasping,
Please get out
before you get hurt.

As she eased behind the wheel
of her battered Subaru Mina glimpsed her petite savior
blocking the exit
& behind that camo'ed arm
the lunging, livid faces
of various military personnel.

Was it a ringing in her ears she heard?
All in all it was
just another brick in the wall.

These words clanged through Mina
            like dumb electricity
    as she played her fingers over her ribs.

                        She felt pain but
                    where was the wound?

Crushing the cigarette underheel
        she watched her tobacco plume rise   rise
                            past the topmost branches
                                    of the white pines
                        past steepletop & contrail
                        past stratosphere

                        toward the Pleiades.

Our Heroine is Born & Brings Dinner

She raged forth from the dark red dark

          & slid into the family tub
      amid the cheers of a welcoming tribe
        of women
       who called themselves the Seven Sisters.

  With a yellow-checked tea towel
  they rubbed the breath into her
  as they rubbed off
  the slick of her journey

      & wrapped her like a baguette.

   Mina said her mother *She must be Mina Kali*

Naming is making & here was a name
       that sat like a crown
       on her soft little head
       but despite its grand sound

Mina is Sanskrit for *fish* & Kali's the goddess of destruction.

        A piranha
        couldn't be better named.

It was the month of topaz & thanks.
             The tom turkey in the yard had become
         an apple-fattened menace
           rushing the fencing
             meant to confine him.

He held his warty head with the jaunty hauteur of the doomed.

    & the leaves of the beech   *yellow yellow yellow*
                                    hushed
                                    in their falling….
while up under the eaves
     her mother gave a final
    sour-breathed heave

                                    as Mina napped
       a swaddled storm in an auntie's arms
                       & the ruby placenta
                  slopped
               into an old bread bowl
     (its gold glaze crazed from years of use)
    & was swiftly delivered
    downstairs to the round kitchen table.

       Mutterkuchen.   Mother-cake.

The Seven Sisters had delivered them before.
       Midwives all
       except for Auntie Anna   the cook
                          who entered the bodies
                         of the Sisters & their children
                    through the work of her hands
                    as peeler, stirrer, kneader, baker.

                 So they partook
                 of her good will
                 & Mina's placenta

because the Maori do
because the Navajo do
because goats & camels do
because it is *natural*
                    though with cups of green tea
                                        & a toast

                            to family unity.

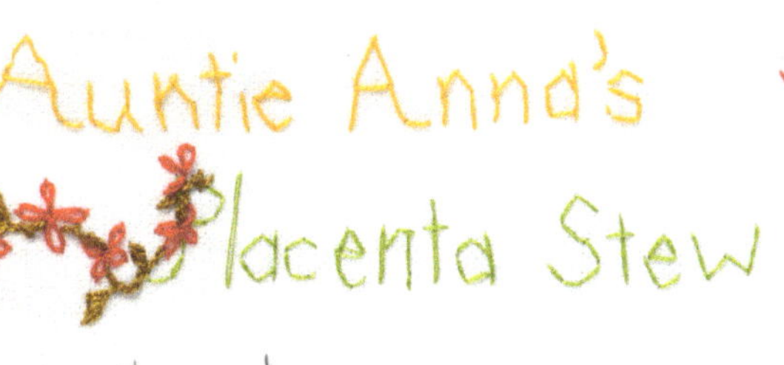

Auntie Anna's
Placenta Stew
basil   celery
thyme   mushshrooms
          rosemary   dice placenta and

Auntie Anna's Placenta Stew

After you wash the placenta, pat it dry and scrape away the membrane.
Let it rest while you stir a mixture of flour (half white, half wheat), a pinch of salt
*   and a few grinds of pepper in a pie plate.*
Cut the placenta into bite-sized pieces and toss them into the flour mixture.
Once they're coated, put them aside to dry; dice celery, carrots and onion.
Slowly cook this trinity in olive oil, and when the onions give up their opacity, add
*   a handful of sliced mushrooms—wild, if you can find them.*
Let the mushrooms release their liquid, and once they have, add the placenta.
Let the placenta brown companionably with vegetables for a few minutes.
Now is the time to add something acidic— a can of tomatoes or a couple glugs of wine.
Pick a handful of herbs, thyme for strength, rosemary for ardor, basil for balance.
Toss these atop the stew and cover it with a loose-fitting lid.
Set the table, clean the kitchen, and when you're ready, the stew will be too.

Mina's Childhood Leaves an Impression

Mina's first three years
        were spent as close as
           close is
    to the two other children
    of the group of women
    who'd been together   since the early 70's
        (a/k/a ancient times)
          at UNH.

In a nest of patched quilts & pillows
        sour-sweet with their spit-up
          set up
         like a whelping basket
         next to the woodstove
  they played, napped
 & occasionally pulled hair
while the beat of 70's mix tapes
lub-dubbed in the background   as a kind of aural wallpaper.

The children were

    Abby   Abenaki Indian   who the aunties had fostered since birth
    Mina   homemade   thanks to an unsuspecting semen donor
    & Malcolm half white/ half black who the aunties called African American
              adopted at 3 months.

To the Seven Sisters   America was a place of violence & injustice
        also a place of opportunity &plenty
  so they took one child
  from each of the ethnic groups
    that interested them most.

Abby   eldest
     walked first

                    leaving Mina & Malcolm
                         creeping far behind
                           often grasping
                         for the same handhold
          on the wobbly kitchen chairs
                 & creaky stairs
                 that led to the bedrooms.

Ambulation earned Abby
     first choice of bedrooms
                 but instead of taking
                 the largest or sunniest
          Abby chose the nook closest
                           to the wing where her aunties slept.

Once all three children
were walking & talking   they were deemed
                                      ready for schooling
          down in the cellar classroom
                 where a ravaged blackboard
                 & five mustard-yellow vinyl chairs
                                 snagged in a Sunday scavenge
                 from the dumpster   behind a Midas muffler shop
                 were arranged in a sacred circle.

From behind a saggy batiked screen
     the old washing machine
          chomped & slurped
     through its weekly cuisine.

This was where the aunties taught the children   everything
                                                      (they thought)
                                                      the children needed
                                                      to know.

        The necessaries   (alphabet, colors & simple math)
                      were taught from the same primers
                                the aunties had been taught from—

        Dick & Jane ran
        & watched Spot run
                across the thick pages
                worn soft & gray as moleskin

                                  though Jane's hair was a bit darker
                                                  a bit curlier
                                  her skin benefitted from
                                     the bronzing melanin
                          of Auntie Jean's ocher Sharpie pen

        (with which she'd chastely edited "Dick"
                        to "Richard.")

Only the Best: A Homemade Scrapbook Primer

The Seven Sisters pooled their expertise
 & found (though it was no surprise to them)
the curriculum in Portsmouth public schools
from kindergarten through the seventh grade
was a ghoulish goulash of misdirected myth—
a litany of skirmishes in swamps
from Maine to Washington, then *westward ho!*
The wagon trains, brute Injuns & the Gold Rush
just a rush to conquer nature, kill the beast
called wilderness. Success—it's wild no more.

The great Midwest's now choked with factory farms
their noxious runoff poisoning the wells.
Monsanto, greedy pitchfork-shaking Satan,
who foisted GMO on soy and corn—
was barely mentioned in New Hampshire texts.
What's next? Omit the fact that Uncle Sam
sold weapons to Iran, Afghanistan?

You could fill a book from those lacunae.
so fill they did— called it their scrapbook primer.
No wars allowed, their textbook spotlit lives
of heroes like Thoreau & Emerson
John Reed & Emma Goldman, socialists
& certain suffragettes, then moving on
to Civil Rights & strangely, the Space Race
(Auntie Nan's obsession), climate change.
They pasted articles from *Mother Jones*,
The Nation, Utne Reader, their local rag—
the venerable *New Hampshire Gazette*,
"the nation's oldest newspaper"™

They bound a dozen copies of these books
with silver plumber's tape in hope that word
would spread from Portsmouth outward to the world.
They'd welcome other classmates so their three
 would have companions. This was not to be.

The Homeschool Curriculum

On the first day
of the first year   of their formal education
the first assignment   was a self-portrait

Abby, Mina & Malcolm
     drew with the black pens
     given them

head hair eyes mouth neck body arms legs…... *ta-da!*

                                        then each was handed
                                        a thick crayon
                                        of the appropriate hue—

"Indian Red" for Abby
                         (since renamed "Chestnut")
"Flesh" for Mina
                         (since renamed "Peach")
"Gray" for Malcolm

                         (a darker tone, "Outer Space"
                         was introduced years later by the manufacturer.)

Once they colored themselves in
          the children were ready for filling
                    like Auntie Anna's pie crusts.

From their small circle
in the classroom
                    each child could see duct-taped to the concrete walls
                              a poster of a hero—

     fierce Che   in his black beret
     Dr. King   peering through his "I Have a Dream" speech
     Angela Davis   cool & defiant

& a poster of "the Movement"—

a tie-died peace banner that had twice marched on Washington
(with a couple of burns from dropped joints
which the children thought
were bullet holes)

a copy of Elizabeth Cady Stanton's <u>Declaration of Sentiments</u>
signed by the women at Seneca Falls.

& a poster that declared:

It'll be a great day
when our day care centers
have all the money they need
and the Navy has to hold a bake sale
to buy battleships.

The First Hints of Mina's Remarkable Aptitude

It was an August so hot & dry
                    the grasshoppers could not   stop   leaping.

                              Each stalk of Indian paintbrush
    (which the children were told to call   Native American paintbrush)
        was orange-burnt   an ember
                        on a poker.

It was a summer stingy with dew—
                    on the days it beaded the grass
            the sun shone so fierce on those convexities
                              it burned the green blades brown
            on the spots where the dew sat
                        before   evaporating.

    Those speckled grasses
                    were good cover
            for all manner of hoppers
                        & a challenge for Mina to catch.

        She needed food for her pet garter snake
                              live food.
        She enjoyed watching
                              the snake's casual outcurling
            & the stunned   useless kicking
                        of its prey.

Mina wondered
why the insects never saw it coming.
                                    After all
                                    they were alone
                                    in a tank
                                    with a snake.

Easygoing Malcolm & Independent Abby

Malcolm   the youngest
                              was happy to catch grasshoppers
              while Mina read in the shade   so eager to be near her
                                          he'd do whatever she asked
                                          he'd fetch her lemonade
                                          he'd do her tasks.

        Abby   had talented hands
                      agreed the aunties   delighted.
                                They'd read
                                          of her tribe's stitchery
                              & hoped
                                          to encourage a propensity
                      for the needle's deft conversation.

        So Abby   hemmed the pants & dresses
                            bought on Bag Day
                                          at the Portsmouth Good Will
                            kept up the button can & the rag bag
                            made change purses for Christmas gifts.

She knitted, appliquéd, crotcheted & bargelloed
                            her way into every auntie's heart.

Mina watched   Abby's fleet fingers
                            her quiet focus
                            her patience   & understood
                                          that by making things
                                          Abby made herself
                                          valuable.

        But Abby's kindness
                      felt like a kind of sloppiness—
                      like one of Auntie Nan's

leaky kisses
after she finished another bottle
of Auntie Anna's May wine—
                    its oozy ways worked against
                    the *us-versus-them* designations
                    with which Mina had grown
                                        so comfortable.

One cool Saturday afternoon
as she chose smooth stones from the driveway
        for the cairn she was constructing
    in her snake's tank
            Mina made up a song:

                                    Abby, Abby, what does she know?
                                            How to quilt and how to sew.
                                    Abby, Abby, who is her friend?
                                        Nobody All she does is mend.
                                    Abby, Abby, needle & thread.
                                            She'll sew & sew until she's dead.

When Malcolm asked to play
        with Mina that day   the price
                            was learning the song
                            which Malcolm chanted gleefully
                            under the flapping paisley sheets
                                            pinned on the clothesline
                                    hung from pine to sugar maple.

He didn't see Auntie Karen
        the disciplinarian
                    & laundry goddess   lay her wicker basket down
        & stand
            hands on ample hips

                                        while Malcolm's pure soprano
                                                rang out
                                    the chorus for a third time.

When he was done
        he was done for—
                Auntie Karen laid into him
                            & sent the boy to his room
                                    without supper.

            At the table that night
            over tempeh tostadas
            a discussion was had
            about the inevitability
            of male aggression.

Further Details on the Children's Education

As in most matters
  the Seven Sisters   decided by committee
             how to educate their children.

    There were Spanish lessons & painting lessons
        social sciences & math
        but English was tricky   (Mina never forgot
                     the arguments about
                     "The Cannon.")

The children had been taught which words
                to omit
                from the Pledge of Allegiance
  & were frankly discouraged
    from singing
    The Star Spangled Banner

      (its glaring rockets & bursting bombs
        were too militaristic
        declared Auntie Sarah
        the group's U.S. history maven.)

Etiquette of a sort
was also taught
    but not the "please pass the peas"
        no boardinghouse reach
        "yes Ma'am" "No Sir"
        manners hammered
        into generations of children.

        The aunties' priority?
        A full-voiced *Speak Truth to Power*
        attitude in their three. Along with a firm handshake
        & the understanding that if arrested a march
        or demonstration (which constituted much of their
        family's social life) all that goes out the window:
                Go limp.

Mina Begins to Have Questions

I have seven moms.
          Who is my dad?

If all whites are racist
            am I racist too?

Why didn't I get a Barbie Dreamhouse for Christmas?

If the police & government can't be trusted
                        why trust my aunties?

I have seven moms.
          Who is my dad?

If religion is for morons
                    why do we recite Reverend King
                    each morning before our muesli?

Why can't I wear my pink tutu outside the house?

If everyone is equal
            why is President Reagan so bad?

Who is my dad?

Abby Blossoms in Middle School

When each child moved into a second decade
    she or he was sent   to the local middle school
                down the mountain
     along with Auntie Emily   a 6th grade math teacher.

    After a breakfast
     of whole oats
     brewer's yeast
     & blackstrap molasses
       (Adelle Davis still had her ghostly finger
           in the family cuisine)
Abby would dress
make herself an almond butter sandwich
   on Auntie Anna's homemade bread
     & wait at the back door
     darning a mitten
     or fixing a rip with a decorative stitch
         until it was time to leave.

                     Rather, she'd be
                     re-crocheting
                     & re-fixing.

  It seemed she'd never finished
  as much as she thought she had.

From 7:25am to 2:05pm
  each weekday
  Abby excelled.
      She was grades ahead
     in reading
        & though quiet
    she was known to be
       quite kind.

       But on weekends & evenings
        Abby occupied a territory

                                        between
                                    ignored & besieged.
                    She'd return home to board games in progress
                                        games that lasted days
                        & which she was not allowed to join
                            because
                "it's not right to start something in the middle."

Imperialism
        the family's favorite
        had been cobbled together
                from a Monopoly board:

            the familiar Atlantic City landmarks
            replaced with global real estate destinations
                            well-known for their struggles
                                against various Imperialisms
                                        through the ages.

Boardwalk & Park Place   became Hong Kong
Mediterranean & Baltic Avenues   were Africa
India   occupied the entire railroad system
the utilities   served as the Phillippines
& everyone agreed that Chance best suited Puerto Rico.

  She or he who returned the most money
                was declared the winner.

    Not that there weren't disputes.

            Auntie Karen, a nonpracticing Jew
                    was so upset
                    when the rest
                voted in the Golan Heights
                        that she "forgot"
                    to put the yeast
                in her bread that week.

Up the stairs Abby would trudge
       to her nook
           tucked up against the aunties' wing
with a snack
               (a whole oat muffin
               spread with apple butter
               or her favorite kale chips)
      curl up on her bed
     & do her homework
          using the required #2 pencil
           & find the next morning
                 random answers   erased.

          Abby took this in stride
              mystified
  & because she was a stubborn one
       began to do homework in pen.

A Small Private Satisfaction

Sipping milky tea
from her yellow mug
Mina smiled: it took
only five minutes
to unravel the sleeve

Abby had knitted
for Auntie Sarah's
fiftieth birthday.

Abby & Mina in Middle School

Mina followed Abby
              to the public middle school
                            after seventh grade

     where Abby had established herself
     as a person who did for others—

she was a guider of wheelchairs
a tutor of English for the refugees
                       from Sudan
                            who'd been sent unluckily
                                             to chilly New England
& an afterschool helper
                   of the beleaguered part-time custodian.

          For teachers & staff   this was reason to smile.
          For Mina   this was provocation.

          Rumors began to circulate—   that Abby was being paid
                                          for her kindnesses

                                          that Abby was a shoplifter
                                          recently released
                                          from reform school.

     Mina reassured Abby's friends:
              Oh no, Abby never shoplifted!
              But she almost grew up
              in a reform school 'cuz her whole family
                            were crazy drunks
              & then my aunties took her in.

Abby's friends, stunned
              didn't quite believe the stories
                   but it was a bit
                   more difficult
                           to fit

                 her
                      at their lunch table

           & a bit
           easier
           to forget
        to invite her
                    to their sleepovers.

             Abby faded from their attention…..

    But Mina
       oh Mina they noticed

                     when she held her nose each time Ms. Thompson
                             whose putrid breath
                         came from bad dental health
                                   passed by her desk

                     when she'd toss Ginger Chew's lunch
                                    into the garbage can
                     chirping
                             "Ginger can't chew today."

    & when she'd hang inside the door
        of the beautiful Ms. Singh
        repeating the same lame joke
                "Shouldn't you be
        a chorus teacher
        not an English teacher?"
    Then Ms. Singh would smile
        & squeeze Mina's shoulder
            & just for a moment
            something in Mina
                would loosen
                    & soften.

One Morning in the Principal's Office at Portsmouth High

—You know why you're here, don't you? Your home room teacher sent you down because he doesn't know what to do with you. Why can't you stand with the others, just stand there while the Pledge is being said? You don't have to put your hand over your heart. Just stand there respectfully. Out of respect for your fellow students if not the flag. But I do have to say, Mina, you're not winning any friends with this kind of behavior.

We Meet Mina's Target

                    Ginger Chew was an awkward girl
                    but there are few things less elegant
                              than a thirteen year old.

          Even Lacey MacNeil

                              student council president
                                   soccer star & an overbrimming 36C
                                   came to school with hair so oily
                    toward the end of the week   that when she moved
                                        suddenly
                                   the acrid mosquito-buzz stink of her hair
                                        floated, fartlike,
                                             through American history class.

          Ginger's glandularity was no worse
     than Lacey's
        or Mina's
                    her clothes no cooler
                         her grades no better

                              but Ginger had a habit
                              of biting her nails
                              down to their bleeding quicks.

          That she did this in class
                         this intimate practice
               in front of her peers
               in the kind of reverie reserved for, say
                                        nose-picking
               infuriated Mina—

                              Gross! What's wrong with her!
                                   Doesn't Ginger know
                                        you do certain things
                                             in private?

     Mina hatched a plan.

nettle

Dear students of Mr. Washington's 5th period English class,

We are pleased to announce a food drive for our fellow student, Ginger Chew.
It has come to our atention that Ginger desparatly needs food so she can keep
growing!! Please save all your nail clippings from fingers and toes from now
until after winter vacation. Ginger cannot live without them!!

From The Crew To Feed Ginger Chew

(The CTFGC)

Mina   who'd been taught to follow through
                                        followed through—

          she saved her nail clippings   finger & toe
               in a discarded amber vial
                    after scratching off her mother's name
                         & the word *Clonazepam*.

                                                  (As she pawed
                                        through the bathroom trash
                                        she found a bounty
                                        of other clippings
                                        & dropped them into the nail vial.
                                        This became her weekly practice.)

Behind the whitewashed clapboards of a dozen Portsmouth houses
behind the bathroom doors of Portsmouth's best addresses
two dozen students saved their filthy sickle-shaped clippings
in a kind of viral violence that thrilled Mina, teen oppressor.

History is Made in American History Class

Ladies & Gentlemen
     & esteemed readers from all parts
  local & far-flung

    on this, the eighth day of January
      Miss Ginger Chew will be honored with

        A LIFETIME SUPPLY

          of the cream of the crop   the top of the heap
            the most delicious   nutritious
          fungus-riddled rinds   it has been Mina's pleasure to collect!

This is a truly stupendous   life-changing
                  gift   wrapped
                       in expensive embossed silver paper
                       saved since last Christmas by none other than
          Abby   who had been pleaded with
                       cajoled & finally bought outright
       with a promise   that Mina would do her chores
                       for the week.

    For an extra week off
      from doing the dishes
      & scooping the litter
  Abby wrapped the shifty little box

                which Ginger discovered
                resting jauntily on her desk
                in history class
                on the Monday after Christmas break.

       Yes, Ladies & Gentlemen
        she opened it
        she opened it so quickly
        & with such high-pitched zeal

that they who did their best
to look elsewhere
to avoid implication
gasped along with Ginger
when the contents of the box
seemed to explode   sending thousands of clippings
                                     sharp   yellowing   shrapnel
                                     onto Ginger   & her neighbors

"Alright Ginger, very funny.
Wipe off your desk.
We've got lots to get to today."   With that, Mr. Washington
                                     launched into his lecture
                                     on Reagan's efforts to unite
                                     the two Germanys.
                                     "Tear down that wall, Mr. Gorbachev!"

*All in all it's just
another brick in the wall…..*

What a chorus, Ladies & Gentlemen, what a moment!

On her long walk home that day
Ginger's breath as it left her lips
became a wheaten bale of shame
tumbling in the weak winter light.

High School: an ode to accretion

It
begins
with a zit
a spray of zits
pus buckshot
bra straps & tits
fried eggs, skeeter bites
cantelopes & headlights
he's got a boner, a stiffy
 a woody, a chubby, a hard-on
she's on the rag, riding a tampon
she's got the curse, the crimson tide, aunt Flo's
visiting, he's rank, he stinks, she's stank, a skanky ho
she's trailer trash, he's nascar, a cracker, a redneck, a hick
that's so gay, she's bi, a rug muncher, a dyke, a lipstick lesbian
he's a faggot, a fairy, a homo, queer, brokeback, light in the loafers, a limp dick
they're lame, losers, tools, dorks, douchebags, morons, pussies, retards & fucktards all.

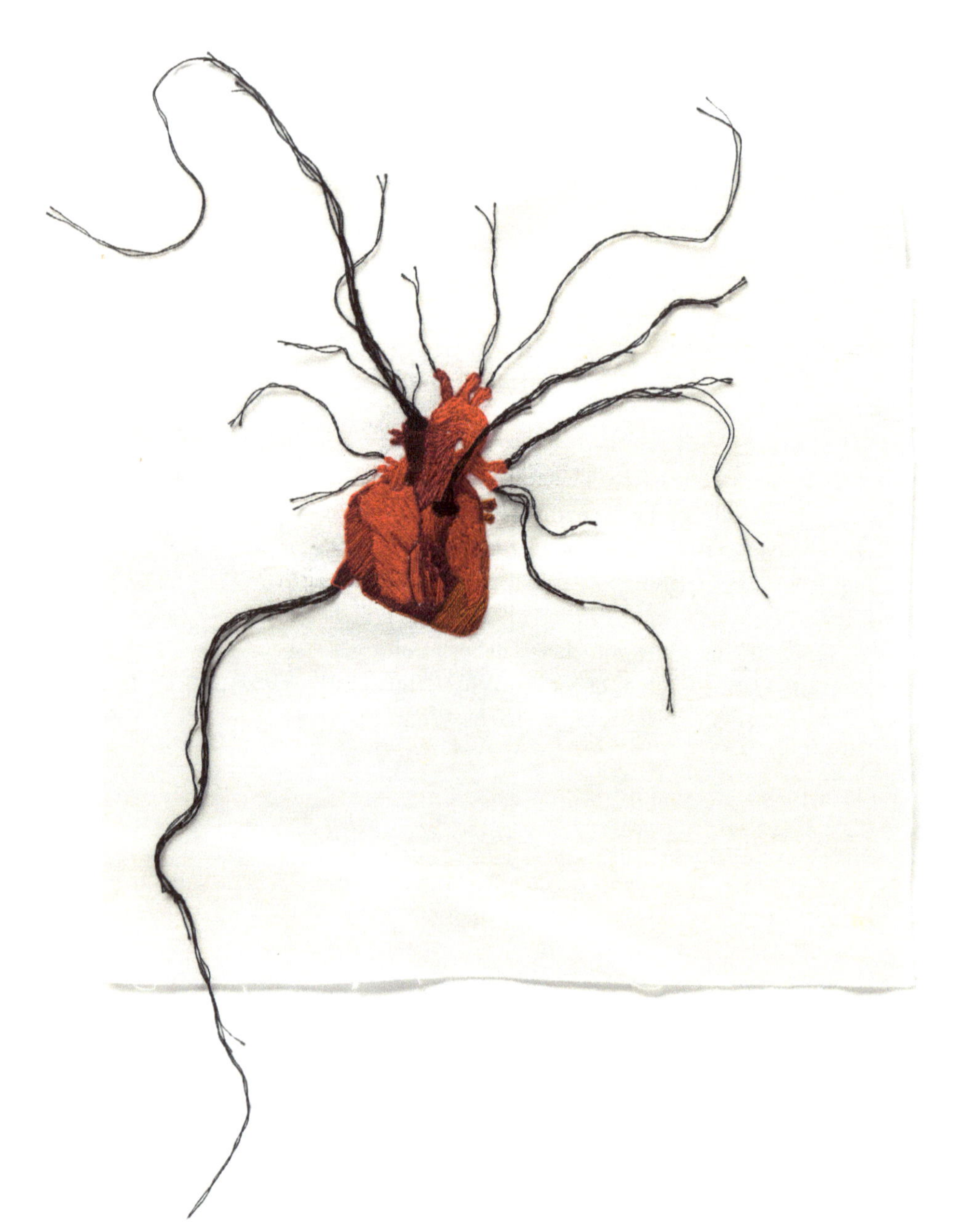

Everyone Faces a Wall Sometime

By the time the tuxes were rented
       & the local florist's fingers
           were blistered from twisting
             the stems
        of 206 chrysanthemum corsages
          in Portsmouth High's   yellow & purple
     each of the Seven Sisters' children
            had a plan
  & each   met a wall
         which blocked that plan.

               Abby's wish to major in fiber arts at RISD
                 was thwarted by family finances.
                 She would take a year off
                    then two   then five
                     & live at home
                  (in fact she'd never leave)
                 saving her paycheck   waiting
                        tables
                   at a local Greek diner
                  & teach weaving
                in continuing ed. classes.

Mina was accepted
by every college
she'd applied to
on the strength
of her SAT analytical score
              & though she intended
               to major in the arts
               the only promise she showed
            was an increasing subtlety
              in the art of
              humiliation:

she'd learned to disguise
her distinctive low voice
during late-night calls
to Ginger's cell phone
asking for appointments
for a mani-pedi &
complimentary massage.

When came his time
to graduate from Portsmouth High
Malcolm   co-captain of the basketball team
who led them to victory
in the New Hampshire state finals
was UNH's #1 recruit.

Malcolm would go on
to make his coaches proud
though he succumbed
to the full court press
of seven determined aunties

(who did not raise a young black man
to become something as racially cliché
as a professional basketball player)

& majored in political science
struggling through economics
both macro & micro
with the help of a tutor.

He would go on
to a steady but unexciting career
as a loan officer
at Portsmouth Savings Bank
spending evenings & weekends
doing what he loved—

coaching the local YMCA basketball team.

Mina on the Bridge

Mina believed she'd never seen otters or mink;
though auntie Jean's car had rumbled over a corpse

one late December afternoon   & Mina thought she knew
the torn bag of fur and gut had once been muskrat.

For days the thermometer's needle had not passed zero.
Mina stopped mid-cross on the footbridge over the river

 to watch two brown commas   (otter   mink   or muskrat?)
race along the icecoast   up deep banks made deeper by snow

& roll down   chittering   into a river   half ice, half water.
Mina wondered whether this was play or war

whether these beasts were grown or growing.
Crossings are their most opaque when we're halfway through.

So she named them mink & called it war
but they were pups at play   & otters.

Mina Attends Vassar

Leave it up to a child   & the decision's made
                                      through a rope course of tangents
                                          (& a few unconscious loop de loos)

      Mina choice of Vassar   one of the Seven Sisters colleges
                                      (also the nick for the Pleiades
                                                    whose stars
                                          wink in the winter heavens
                              & in whom Mina always saw an arrow in flight)

            was a source of amusement & relief to the aunties
                  who had been stumped by Mina's antics
                  & had a vague sense of guilt
                  they explained away
                  through her father's probable
                        genetic shortcomings.

Mina studied   Plath Virgil Derrida
     played   beer pong chess   viola
   observed   Kwanzaa Earth Day Ramadan.

                              She gave up   Cheez Doodles   white food
                                    & eating anything with eyelashes.

She protested America's corporate culture
      by forgoing toothpaste   shampoo   & deodorant.

She saved water by not doing laundry
        & following the *if it's yellow* edict.

                Thus Mina's consciousness expanded   expanded
                                                & again expanded
        until her roommate grew intolerable
                then the other students
        & even her professors
                except Dr. Randolph
                        who was   intolerable to begin with.

    Eventually Mina avoided
        the public spaces
        the libraries
            & lecture halls
            occupied as they were by losers.

        By November
        she existed on
        other students'
            lecture notes
        in exchange for
        her special popcorn
        which was vegan
        & vaguely Indonesian.

                This worked well for her classmates too—
                    the consensus among them
                    was that Mina was on the verge of
                    a crack-up.

                They could smell it on her.

Mina's Spicy Popcorn

*Buy the freshest organic Native American corn available. Pop half a cup
of it in an air popper. While you're waiting for the corn to pop, stir
together a teaspoon of sriracha, a teaspoon of ground turmeric &
a tablespoon of oil, preferably canola. When the popcorn is done popping,
put it in a large bowl. Pour the oil & spice mixture over it. Toss it together.
Add coarse kosher salt if you need it, but you shouldn't.*

Mina Marches Forth

Home on fall break   the Seven Sisters' Thanksgiving table
                 thought Mina
           was clearly   a desecration
               of Native American culture
                 native American birds
                     & the cranberry.

Where did Abby stand on this?
How about Malcolm?
Clearly brainwashed. Clearly.

Those women—aunties, *ha!*— understood nothing
                 of the world outside
                 the one they'd made
                 for their children.
       They were too busy
          serving the meal
          washing the dishes
          & wrapping up leftovers.

Disgusted with the bourgeois bonds of domesticity
            their repetitiveness
         & the distinct whiff of subservience
           of those so-called radical warrior women

       Mina bought herself a pair of boots
     (black)   (of repurposed tires)
with $127 she lifted
from Auntie Jean's purse
         & marched bravely into her future.

Mina Decides to Become an Artist

Mina had squeezed the lemon of Vassar
        all she could
          & the fact that no one would room with her
             —sure, it was a small issue—
           was a sign she was once again
              misunderstood.

It was time for making
    time for gathering
          into her grasp
          all the tools of brass & wood
             water & bristle
             leather & stone
      that every star of history or
     the solitary arts was famous for.

        In a post-Thanksgiving flurry
            of repurposing
Mina roasted the bones of a flightless bird
& boiled them with fennel & nutmeg
down to a rich broth
       & drank it for courage.

      Broth made from bones is strengthening.

She learned to throw pots
    (& though disappointed there was no *real* throwing)
      Mina proved an apt potter
     of pitchers
    with golden glazes
     until she tired of pottery.

Music
amused her.   But she had the voice of a bullhorn
         & knew it
         so she tried the flute
         & flailed. & failed.

Then a brush with paint & canvas—
                    but the figure escaped her
                            (or rather   the face
                                which always required the same old
                                                four features:
                                eye   eye   nose   mouth)

So she tried still lifes
        & titled them   (because naming, too, is making)
        Citron Feather & Crown
            I II III IV V VI etc…

But in each she saw
 an unalterable flaw
        & each one she burned.

                            We destroy what we don't understand
                            & hope the fear that accompanies
                                our sense of not-knowing
                                        leaves us as well

    —rising like some sort of smoke to some sort of heaven
                where some sort of filter
                        recycles it
                for some kind of future.

Once she'd thrown them all into a dented barrel
                    & touched   the tongue
                                of a lit match
                                to the corner of the topmost canvas
        Mina watched
                    as an eighth-acre of Tyrian purple
                                & yellow ochre
                                        curled
                            from the canvases

                                & came
                                at last
                                to life.

Mina Has a Revelation

As she watched the paint darken & lift
                ember-edged
                into the January sky
                Mina understood that she was not
                                destined
                to be an artist.

  With this insight
& a vague sense of relief
   Mina took a trip back home to New Hampshire
                driving her little yolk-colored Subaru
                                straight through
        from Manhattan
                    past suburbs   sooty cities
                        over state lines
                                past a few spectacular glimpses
                        of the Atlantic &
                                    the scrubby collar of cattails
                            that filters
                            the earth from the earth.

A Brief but Eventful Visit Home

The house at the top of the hill
            the house Mina called home
                looked reassuringly familiar—

                    streaks of pine sap
                        still ran like honey
                    down the north face of the house
            & a small gray satellite dish
                        had replaced the rusty antenna.

        She walked into the kitchen
    where a few bushels of bruised & lumpy apples
    sat on the cracked linoleum floor
                & Auntie Anna's canning paraphernalia
                lay on the table.

            Auntie Karen tromped up from the basement
            with a load of wet laundry to be hung.

                Auntie Anna   Mina was told   was upstairs resting
                but Abby would be home soon
                            from the co-op
                                with the groceries.

    That night six aunties squeezed around the stained oak table
                with their two daughters
                    (auntie Emily had left the year before
                    to pursue her dream:
                    a doctorate in critical theory)
                reminiscing over bowls of root vegetable stew
                            & Abby's applesauce
                        when a small
                        purring kitten
                        curled between
                            Mina's
                        sternum & heart.

Mina slept fitfully
   in the wing chair in the parlor—
        the bedroom she'd shared with Malcolm
          had become Abby's craft room—

rising before dawn
     to the uneven tock-tock of the mantel clock
    & the intermittent call of a barred owl:

      who cooks for you?
      who cooks for you all?

        She was back
        in Manhattan
        before the
        glass carafe
        had auto-filled
        with coffee.

Discipline in Lemon Chiffon

Once it occurred to her that she was no artist
Mina found time for small pleasures—
    decorating her apartment
   & cooking her own meals.
A month of trials & she mastered
  the chard soufflé; two months
& she'd become a baker
   of gluten-free muffins.

    But the night
she learned that Auntie Anna's exhaustion
  was M.S.
she walked the fifty-nine blocks
    to Bleecker
& bought herself two pricey lemon cupcakes
—Anna's favorite.

   When her headache
   resolved
Mina thought *I can learn to make these.*

Sugar-flour-butter-egg-lemon
   & a pinch of cream of tartar
    to steady
   the delicate crumb.

The ingredients are simple
the discipline difficult.

   Seven weeks
   & then success—
Mina made something
   to be proud of.

Mina Gets the Mail

Those weeks of culinary experimentation
left Mina scrambling to cover
her May obligations.

She found among the bills & catalogues
in her post office box
a letter from Auntie Sarah:

Dear M,
Didn't you know this girl?
So sorry. Suicide.
Your Auntie S.

A folded rectangle
torn from *The Portsmouth Herald*
fluttered to the floor:

Xia "Ginger" Chew, 20… beloved daughter of Li and Zhu Chu…. departed this earth on April
19…predeceased by her younger brother Ming "Matthew" Chew….who died at the hands of a
group of thugs….Ginger is survived by the teens she mentored…

…emigrated from China with her parents as an infant. …proud graduate of Portsmouth High
School…..studying criminal justice at Portsmouth Community College.

A graveside service ….followed by a Celebration… at All Souls Unitarian Universalist…
Calling hours will be held from…donations in her memory to The Ginger & Matthew Chew
Foundation…consider volunteering….

Some would shake their heads
Some would burst into tears
Some would look upward
Some would collapse

Some would shudder
Some would feel guilt
Some would call the family
Some would wonder if they'd played a part

    Not Mina

    though she wrote a check
    with a note:

        in memory of Ginger.

Ginger Chew

Love Finds Mina Kali

Look through a telescope   you find galaxies
         those whirling ellipses held fast
            by attraction.

       But to find love?
    Even a thicket of telescopes
            their black legs flamingoed
             at the window
     their Galilean monocles
       are blind to it.

Mina had her share
    of romances—

     a high school steady (five full weeks)
       with a boy named Om

     winter break with a chain-smoking rugger
       from Australia or New Zealand
        she couldn't remember

& a brutal semester of desk sex
    with an African American assistant professor of art history
    followed by his withdrawal
    of an offer for a grad school recommendation
      & nine nights
       of recrimination dreams.

    Men & their half-erect nonsense.

She vowed a year of celibacy
       though   within the span of the moon's wane
            love found her
         & love fell hard
       as did Mina   hard
         & wholly.

Tricks & Treats

Invited to a Halloween party
at the Park Slope brownstone
            of a famous painter   once Mina's studio art professor
            & her famously wealthy husband
                        (owner of three galleries)
                        (owner of the walls of three galleries)
                        (owner of the art on the walls of three galleries)

Mina   an aspiring fashion designer
                            for a semester
                        went dressed as a canary yellow glowstick.
        A nod to rave culture?
        An homage to trick-or-treaters?
                        She didn't know
                        but she made an impression
                        on the tranny Cleopatra whose diamante diadem
                                    put Liz Taylor to shame
                        & the old fart trying to pass as a hippie.

                        Time for a smoke in the huddle on the deck
                        & yes   the Pleiades were twinkling.

From the shadows   stepped a handsome "soldier"
                        sporting fatigues & a ginger buzz cut:
                            -got an extra?
                            -got a light?
                            -got a name?

            Violet.

            The topaz studs
            in Violet's ears
            winked like
            small cats
            waking.

Here the certain attraction.
Here the flicker of recognition.
Here the bow's draw
                    the sting & ecstatic wound   the hit &
                                                    mutual fall.
Here the *yes*.

Does conversation matter when the meaning was unspoken?

                                        They tapped each other's
                                        contact info
                                        into personal
                                        communication devices
                                        made plans
                                        for brunch the following day.
                                        Made out.

Mina gussied up for brunch
                    pulling on her best black turtleneck
        her near-clean jeans   tucked into black boots
                        (the toes upturned with wear.)

                    First to arrive   she smoked a quickie
                                flicked it
                                sat
                                sipped an o.j.

When in walked Violet
        Sergeant Violet
                        in fatigues.
Sometimes a costume is not a
        cool
        ironic
        antiwar statement
                but a uniform worn proudly
                    for service done willingly.

    Mina resisted the urge to bolt
                & holding the plasticized menu like a shield
                        ordered a boiled egg
                        tea   wheat toast
                        with orange marmalade.

She collected herself
                mouthing a silent *what the hell?*
        behind the menu's flimsy cardboard wall
                took a breath
                & then met Violet's golden eyes.
                Mina met the yes in those eyes.

Over that brunch
over the course
of a cool November Sunday
        & the weeks that followed
                of the year's shortening wick
                        this love was lit.
Mina loves Violet loves Mina

        The eyes of the beloved
        either elevate reflection   or ignore it outright.

    For Mina   they let down that guard
                they tore down her walls
                they invited her to play
    & when she played   too rough
                Violet called her on it.

                Knock it off
                        when Mina leaned over & imitated
                                a server's lisp at the pizza place.
                Knock it off
                        when Mina screamed "asshole" at
                                a passing cabbie who yelled "Dykes!"
                Knock it off
                        When Mina muttered about the mayor
                                the sidewalk garbage, her bakery job.

        Violet had no varnish
                no veneer.

            She was true
                    & in being so   loved truly
                    as she herself had been loved
                    by a widowed father
                    never too tired from his third shift
                                second job
                    to check Violet's homework

                        & recite to her in his raspy lilt
                          the lines he'd been taught
                           as a child in Kilkenny:

Gently touch a nettle and it'll sting you for your pains
Grasp it as a lad of mettle and soft as silk remains.

      She loved Mina with a kind of swaddle
          meant at first for babies, cattle.
      When Mina tested Violet's mettle
          closer holding won the battle.

        Mina began to show herself
            in fits & starts
           worrying that Violet
      might turn from her in disgust.
      But sooner or later never arrived——
      Violet earned Mina's trust.

She loved the 5 year old discouraged from wearing clothes deemed
                          "too gender-identified"

      the 9 year old who asked to learn to cook
                          & was told she was clumsy

      the 13 year old made to stand in the Principal's office
                          each morning while the other students
                          recited the Pledge that she'd been taught
                          was morally wrong.

How to Love a Loaded Gun

A good soldier
knows the
limitations
of her weapons
the right reasons
for their use
& how to
disassemble them.

Domestic Rest

Mina found a small apartment
            a few blocks from Westover Air Force base
            where Violet was stationed——

the third floor of a narrow but tidy home
            owned by a local police officer
& her husband
who despite his disability   (he'd broken his back in a fall
            at the ironworks in Bath)
helped Mina push a dusty four-piece sectional
            she'd found in the dumpster
            out behind the pink brick medical building
            (some habits can't be broken)

up up up three flights of stairs
            to the square living room with its western view
                        of the base
                        & the Berkshires.

The Kims were happy
            to have   not only her rent
                        but the scent
            of Mina's culinary experiments
                        on the harvest gold 70's era stove
                                    which ranged
from beet soup to banana pudding to *bi bim bap*
                        the last
                        a bit worrisome
                        being a Korean dish
            & thus potentially politically inappropriate
                        but Violet reassured Mina
                                    it's enjoyed on both sides of the DMZ.

Mina's Golden Beet Soup

Choose ten taut golden beets. Wash them, then trim their green tresses & set them aside for a salad. Peel your beets, then chop them into small cubes. Do the same to two yellow onions. Cut from a hand of fresh ginger root a piece the size of the tip of your thumb. Peel & chop this very finely. Take an orange & grate all its fragrant peel into a small pile of filament.

Now set a large pot over the flame on your stove & melt a half stick of sweet butter. Scoop all you've chopped & grated into the pot. Cover the pot & let it simmer, stirring every few minutes, for a quarter hour. Pour in seven cups or more of chicken broth. Add the juice of that orange whose peel you've grated. Cover the pot again & let it simmer for an hour. Then let the mixture rest uncovered to cool.

Whir a ladle or two at a time in a food processor until it's velvet smooth. Add a teaspoon of cider vinegar & a pinch of cayenne. Taste your soup for need of salt & pepper. Return it to the pot and heat it gently.

This Should Have Been a Honeymoon

                Each month
        their life on the third floor of the
                                        narrow house
                                                grew a bit
                easier   as Mina & Violet settled into a routine.

Once Violet left for her job on the base
where she worked as a logistics officer
Mina would sit at the small table
they'd bought at a yard sale
& with a cup of milky tea at her elbow
she'd make a list
                of things that needed doing: *clean bathroom*
                                                        pay water bill
                                                        co-op volunteer day
                                                        buy bones for soup

        This arrangement
        —Mina in charge of the house while Violet worked—
                        became their private joke
        —so much for degendering their household tasks—

        Why don't we make it official & get married?
                        said Violet one April morning
                                as she brushed a dusting of snow
                        from the bedroom windowsill
                                before topping off the bird feeder.

Mina smiled
adding it to her list: *get married*
but Violet persisted, *I'm not kidding.*

                                        Violet had just received orders
                                                for redeployment.
                                Having served in Korea
                                & briefly in Iraq   she sensed
                                        that a tour in Afghanistan
                (some of the troops were calling it "Operation Enduring Operation")

                                        would be her toughest.

            All summer & through the fall
            Mina & Violet spent their days
                        in the kind of cram-it-all-in busyness
                    well-known to members of the Armed Forces
                        on the threshold of deployment.

Violet cajoled & cajoled & cajoled
        laying out the case for marriage
        but Mina would have none of it:
                        *Marriage is the licensing
                                of private life.*

                        We must fight to maintain our freedom!
                        Separation of church & state.
                        There should be some kind of partition
                                some kind of wall…

                        Oh.

        On December 4th
        three days after the President announced
        a troop surge   of thirty thousand
        Violet was deployed to Afghanistan.

                    On December 13
        after less than two weeks in Afghanistan
        Violet was killed.

Two Officers at the Door

Two officers at the door.

       Something about a convoy
         an IED

       something about immediately

         no suffering

MINA ALONE

Mina Alone

All right   All right   All right

Mina murmured again & again
              as she spooned up a bit of rice
              from the little pot
              Mrs. Kim had left on her doorstep

              as she turned off the shower & reached
              for the yellow towel   one of the pair
              that she & Violet had bought at the PX
              during their last shopping trip. *All right*

              All right   All right
              as she gasped at the towel's rough embrace
              Her skin hurt.   *All right*

     All right   on Christmas eve
     All right   on Christmas day
     All right   on New Year's eve
     All right   on New Year's day
     All right   on Wednesday Thursday Friday Saturday
                             Sunday Monday Tuesday
     All right   another week & yet another

                 Five months of *all rights*
                    then Mina dialed the phone
                    that rang in the kitchen
                       of a small house in Portsmouth

              Hello? said Mina, *Hello?*

Cast Out from the Pleiades

—Well hello. It's been quite a while since we've talked. No you can't speak to
Auntie Anna. Why? Because Auntie Nan drove her to the doctor. She's not
doing well, Mina. I've had to step in and take care of the cooking. And the
shopping. And the laundry after Auntie Karen separated her shoulder. Yes,
she slipped on the ice. Months ago. Of course Malcolm's been helping. Well I'm
very sorry to hear your news. I liked Violet, but things here are so chaotic that
I don't think it's a good idea for you to come back to Portsmouth. I've got
everything under control. Yeah, you too. Bye.

Coda

The way of grief's the closing of a shutter
a camera obscura; a galaxy
of pinhole truths revealed, likenesses subtler
than the stars. Out from the Pleiades
our Mina wandered, out from the boundaries
of righteous dogma she had mined for malice.
That she'd found passion almost undid Abby
who found herself at thirty——nursemaid, manless.

The good can flounder. Who said the world was just?
The lens has cast it image upside down
but accurately——no detail's lost.
Perhaps what's gone around has come around.
A cruelty like Mina's was only——& best
tempered by her love for Violet.

NOTES

*"Gently touch a nettle and it'll sting you for your pains
   Grasp it as a lad of mettle and soft as silk remains."*
                    —Sixteenth century English proverb

References are made to the song "Another Brick in the Wall (Part II)" by Pink Floyd.

"Galilean monocles" refers to the fact that Galileo invented the telescope.

On December 1st, 2009, President Barack Obama ordered a controversial "troop surge" of thirty thousand American soldiers into Afghanistan.

Matthew Chew was a young artist jumped by a group of six young men on the evening of October 29th, 2010 in New London, CT as he walked home from his job at a pizzeria. He was stabbed to death.

Ginger Chews are a popular sweet and the winner of Fiery Food Association's Scovie Award for Best Candy.

ABOUT THE AUTHOR

Leslie McGrath's interviews with poets appear regularly in *The Writer's Chronicle*. Winner of the 2004 Pablo Neruda Prize for poetry, she is the author of *Opulent Hunger, Opulent Rage* (2009), a poetry collection, and two chapbooks: *Toward Anguish* (2007) and *By the Windpipe* (2014.) Her poems have appeared in *The Awl*, *Agni*, *The Common*, *Slate*, and elsewhere. She teaches creative writing and literature at Central Connecticut State University, and is series editor of *The Tenth Gate*, a new poetry imprint of The Word Works press.

ABOUT THE ARTIST

Rachel May is a writer and teacher who lives in New England. Her book, *Quilting with a Modern Slant*, was published in January 2014 and named a "Best Book of 2014" by *Library Journal* and Amazon.com (in two categories). The book has been favorably reviewed in *The Chicago Tribune, Publisher's Weekly, The Library Journal* (starred), *The Los Angeles Times, The Providence Journal*, and *MarthaStewartLiving.com*. In addition to her work in *Women Born with Fur* and *Out from the Pleiades*, a book of sewn images and fiction is forthcoming from Dusie Press in March 2015. She's recently finished a novel and is at work on a research project focusing on a quilt made between 1830 and 1950. Her writing has been twice nominated for the Pushcart Prize, won several awards and been noted in over a dozen contests. Work has recently appeared or is forthcoming in *Michigan Quarterly Review (and featured as cover image), New Delta Review, Cream City Review, Word for / Word, Indiana Review, The Literary Review, Green Mountains Review*, and other journals. She's been a resident and fellow at The Vermont Studio Center and The Millay Colony.

Look for more Blue Bustard novellas at Jaded Ibis Productions

jadedibisproductions.com/blue-bustard